Killer Finds

An Antique Hunters Mystery Book 3

by

Vicki Vass

Copyright 2017 by Vicki Vass

For information, email Vicki Vass, vicki@vickivass.com or visit our website at: vickivass.com

ISBN: 978-0-9989893-3-4
Printed in the United States of America

Cover design by Paula Ellenberger
www.paulaellenberger.com

10 9 8 7 6 5 4 3 2 1

This book is dedicated to my best friends and antique hunting adventurers, the real Anne and CC, whose true life adventures are stranger than fiction.

Chapter One

Anne sank back onto the plush seat of the Boeing 767, cradling the champagne glass in her hand. Real glass, not plastic. She watched as the other passengers filed past her, dragging their rolling suitcases through the narrow aisle. She was reveling in the luxury. It was her second time in first class, and she definitely could get used to this way of travel. She waved at her best friend, CC, as she walked past. Anne had offered to buy her friend the adjacent first-class seat but CC was too practical to spend that much money. Coach was fine for her, she'd said.

Polishing off the champagne, Anne sat back and relaxed. She was heading home to Chicago. Paris would soon be a fading memory. The past few weeks had been a whirlwind of antique shops, flea markets and French food. Anne waved to the flight attendant. "Could you bring me some more of those little profiteroles?" As the attendant started walking away, Anne stopped her. "Oh." Anne waved her empty champagne flute.

The flight attendant brought over a silver tray filled with the delicate French pastries. She refilled Anne's champagne flute. Anne lifted her glass and nodded at Betsy Buttersworth, who was sitting across the aisle from her. Buttersworth was usually a sticky problem for Anne, but not so much this trip. A truce had been struck with her long-time antique hunting nemesis in the light of great food and fabulous shopping. "Buttersworth," she whispered. Betsy Buttersworth had proved to be an adequate tour guide in Paris for Anne and CC. The two friends—or Spoon Sisters as they were known on their antique hunting blog—shared a love for antiques, shopping and each other. Betsy, on the other hand, acquired antiques for a much less altruistic reason. To her, they were acquisitions to brighten her empty life. With the loss of her fiancé, Betsy had flown to Paris to put a Band-Aid on her broken heart.

Anne and CC hadn't meant to follow her but a sudden windfall allowed Anne the means to treat her best friend and herself to a trip overseas. Betsy nodded back from across the aisle and closed her eyes, leaning back in her luxurious seat. Anne was way too excited. She was running through a mental checklist of her purchases: full-length gilded mirror, check; 17th century armoire, check; ivory and amethyst bangle bracelet, check; 18th century fainting couch, check. She reached into her large orange Prada bag and pulled out one of her notebooks, running a finger down a list of antique hunting requests from blog fans. She hesitated, not sure she was ready to part with some of her finds. She also pictured where she could place the antiques in her overcrowded Chicago bungalow.

As she continued her mental list, a well-dressed man rushed onto the plane and plopped down in the seat next to her. The seat wiggled a bit from his girth. Anne couldn't imagine him fitting back in coach. Either way he looked like he could afford the seat and so did she as she admired her vintage black cashmere Balenciaga dress. She had bought it when she first arrived in France and several seven-course meals later, she wished she would have found it in a larger size. The well-dressed man next to her pulled a handkerchief from his suit jacket pocket and wiped his brow. He was still breathing heavily from running onto the plane. Anne gave him an approving smile. A "look at us, we're in first class" smile. He nodded back politely. The flight attendant walked the aisle preparing passengers for takeoff. The well-dressed man struggled with his seat belt but managed in the nick of time to click it. As the engines revved, the man clenched the handle of his satchel. He shut his eyes tightly. He was still sweating.

As the plane took to the air, he grabbed onto Anne's hand, which was on her armrest, squeezing it tightly. She noticed the vintage Timex watch on his wrist. *Maybe he didn't belong in first class*, she thought. "Are you okay?" she asked.

He turned, staring at her, eyes wide open, not saying a word. The plane continued its ascent and so did the well-dressed man's blood pressure it seemed. His face was bright red. "Should I call the flight attendant?" Anne asked. Still no answer.

After what seemed like longer than it was, the pilot announced that passengers were free to move about the cabin. The seatbelt light turned off and the well-dressed man released his death grip on Anne. He took a deep breath. "I'm so sorry, miss."

Anne thought about the length of the flight. There had to be at least another six, maybe seven hours, left. He maintained his grip on his leather satchel with both hands. "There's room overhead if you want to put your carry-on up there."

He turned and yelled, "No!" scaring Anne. Then he apologized. "I'm sorry. I'm a little nervous. I'm fine. I want to hold the bag."

Anne glanced at the bag. It wasn't much of a satchel, decent second-grade leather, a walnut handle, not vintage. Not even really worthy of first class. The flight attendant came over. The well-dressed man ordered a double scotch. "My name is Anne Hillstrom," Anne told him.

"I'm Bernie." He nodded his head, not releasing his grip from the bag.

"Business or pleasure?" she asked.

"What? What'd you say?" he replied.

"Paris. Were you there on business or pleasure?"

"Yes." He downed his double scotch and ordered another. An hour went by.

Back in coach, CC sat squeezed in between a very tall man typing away on his laptop and a young woman holding her petite Chihuahua on her lap. She had told CC it was her emotional support companion to ease her anxiety about flying. The dog looked quite anxious, shaking, eyes bulging. CC thought her Chihuahua needed an emotional support companion of its own. It would have to be smaller to fit in a smaller carrier. Perhaps a rabbit or a guinea pig. CC did the endless math in her head as she pictured each therapy pet needing a therapy pet and so on. Then the young woman would have to care for each of those pets. Imagine her anxiety then. CC pulled out her iPad, connected to the plane's WiFi and typed her newest blog post, "Dear Friends: Anne and I had a wonderful time in Paris. We saw many sights including the Louvre, Versailles and the Eiffel Tower. I mentioned to the curator at the Louvre that I was an artist myself. He was kind enough to take me on a behind the scenes tour. It was fascinating and I can't wait to share more with you. I shared with him my analogy, comparing my writing to that of a sculptor; only I am shaping words, trimming words from blocks of ideas into sculpted stories. I also had the opportunity to do a day study with Jacques Lamour, a prominent Parisian sculptor. I'm happy to relay that Betsy Buttersworth seems to be healed. The events of the last couple months, as you, dear readers, know, have been hard on her. Thank you for your well wishes. Betsy enjoyed shopping on the Champs-Elysees while Anne scoured the antique stores and flea markets to find many items on our list. Here are some pictures of recent finds from an art school, a very famous local institution that was home to many 19th century painters. Anne was particularly excited about the drawing desk along with the 19th century paintbrushes, easels and palettes she found there. I felt right at home because, as many of you know, I dabble in the arts." CC added pictures of their art school purchases to the blog post.

Then she continued, "I must say that Anne and Betsy got along quite well even when they argued over a pair of 1980 Gaultier-layered fringe pants. Pants. Betsy had her revenge. She won this pair." CC clicked on the image of Anne and her 1960s vintage flowered Capri pants once owned by a Hollywood starlet. "And you all remember that epic battle between Anne and Betsy at Nancy Packwell's estate sale over the pants," CC typed. "I will write more of our adventures once we are back home in Chicago. Until then, au revoir." CC turned the iPad off, adjusting her position. The tall man's arm had found its way into her side, his bony knees scraped the seatback in front, making an annoying sound. She moved slightly closer to the young woman and was face to face with the therapy Chihuahua which was baring its teeth. CC backed away.

She settled back for the long flight, closing her eyes. She drifted off thinking about Brent, her Nashville fling. The young Brad Pitt, Thelma and Louise version. She had called him several times from the St. George in Paris but couldn't reach him. She only allowed herself three messages. That was her line in the sand for relationships, casual or not. If they wouldn't take the time to contact her back after three messages, they weren't worth her time either. She wasn't angry at Brent. In fact, she was grateful. She needed to feel young again, not that 40 was old. After a failed 15-year marriage, the road-hard journalist needed a fling. She fell asleep to the imaginary country music playing in her head.

Up front, Anne leaned her seat back and closed her eyes too. She was about to fall asleep when she felt a sudden drop like a roller coaster. Bernie grabbed her arm and screamed. The lights in the cabin blinked, then went out. Bernie screamed louder. The plane dropped and jostled around. Through the window, Anne saw flashes of white, lighting up the sky. The captain turned on the seatbelt sign. "We've hit some turbulence. Everything is fine. Please remain seated," he said.

Bernie dropped his satchel on the floor. He struggled with his seatbelt, not being able to reach his bag. Two flight attendants rushed up to him. Anne reached for her bag which had fallen to the floor. She dangled her foot around the floor, desperately trying to reach around to see if anything had fallen out. She tried to unclick her seatbelt, but the flight attendant stopped her. "Please, both of you, remain seated," she said.

"My bag, my bag," Anne said.

"My bag," Bernie said.

The flight attendant helped Anne and Bernie retrieve the bags. Just then, the plane dropped again and the flight attendant fell into the aisle. When the lights came back on, Bernie was still shouting hysterically. "Sir, you need to calm down," the flight attendant said.

Bernie turned face to face with Anne, his eyes wild with terror. And then a hand reached over the seat, pushing down on Bernie's shoulder. The co-pilot, wearing his navy blue uniform, spoke in a calm voice, "If you don't settle down, I'm going to have to restrain you. Do you understand?"

"I'm okay. I'll be fine." Bernie said.

The co-pilot looked at the flight attendant. "There's an air marshal deadheading back in coach. Any more problems from this passenger, go get him." She nodded.

The co-pilot went back to the cockpit. Bernie let out another scream as the plane dipped again. He constantly glanced over his shoulder as if looking for someone. "No!" Bernie screamed, jumping up out of his seat and running down the aisle.

Anne swiveled her head around in time to see Bernie run into and apparently lock himself in the lavatory. The flight attendant pounded on the door and then walked back through the curtains into coach. The plane dipped. Anne closed her eyes and stuck her earbuds in. This flight was not as pleasant as the one *to* Paris. She clutched her armrests. Outside her window, thunder crashed. She jumped and closed the shutter on the window. She listened as the furniture appraiser on the *Antiques Roadshow* podcast explained how to authenticate a genuine Chippendale chair, information she would lock away for future reference.

After a while, she glanced at the empty seat next to hers and unclicked her belt. She hurried down the aisle. "Bernie, are you okay?" she asked as she pounded on the lavatory door. The plane swayed under her feet. The overhead lights flickered.

The plane made a hard left. Anne fell against the wall and the lavatory door burst open. Bernie burst out and onto Anne. She screamed, struggling to get out from under his weight.

The flight attendant came rushing and pulled Bernie off of her. She checked his pulse and looked at Anne. Bernie was gone. As Anne stood up, she noticed a gash in Bernie's head. The flight attendant took a cloth napkin and patted the blood. Then she grabbed Anne and escorted her back to her seat. "Miss Hillstrom, you need to stay in your seat."

Once the turbulence had settled, the seatbelt sign turned off and the captain announced that the weather had cleared up.

CC ran up to Anne and sat down next to her. "Are you okay, Anne?"

"I'm not okay." Anne stared straight ahead, trying to push the image of Bernie out of her mind.

"Everything's fine now, Anne." CC patted her hand. "I checked the weather before we left. I knew there was a possibility of storms over the Atlantic. The lightning must have caused a short in the electrical system but don't worry, Anne, the 767 is fine. I did a story about airplane grade aluminum, and it's stronger than ever."

Anne looked out her window as another flash of light crashed around the sky. "Blood, CC, blood. Bernie must have hit his head. He's dead. At least I think he's dead."

For the first time, CC noticed the splotches of red hidden in the black fibers of Anne's vintage dress. "Who's Bernie?"

Before Anne could answer, the flight attendant came back up to them. "Ma'am, I need you to return to your seat," she said to CC.

"Will you be okay?" CC asked Anne, standing up.

Anne nodded. After CC left, the flight attendant sat down next to Anne. "Miss Hillstrom, we have a medical emergency."

"It's Bernie, isn't it?" Anne blurted out.

The flight attendant shushed her. "Miss Hillstrom, please, keep it down," she whispered. "Yes, Bernie passed."

Anne gasped. "Horrible," she whispered.

"Miss Hillstrom?"

"Yes?"

"We have a full flight."

"Yes, I know."

"Miss Hillstrom, you don't understand." The flight attendant leaned over and whispered in Anne's ear. "We have no place to keep the body until we land."

"You can't leave him on the floor outside the lavatory. What if someone needs to—?" Anne paused. "Wait, you're not saying—?"

"The air marshal said he would switch seats with you if you were uncomfortable with the idea."

Anne thought for a moment. "Where's his seat?"

"He's in the last row in coach."

Anne pictured endless glasses of champagne, more profiteroles. Dinner; it would be dinnertime soon. And her luxurious seat that reclined all the way back. Then she thought about being crammed into a tiny seat back in coach. And, she had already picked out a couple movies to watch. "No, I'm okay with staying here."

It took three flight attendants to carry Bernie back to his seat. They strapped him in tight and wrapped a blanket around him. The flight attendant reached over Anne's head and turned off the overhead lights. She gave Anne one last concerned look and walked away.

Bernie's head toppled over and fell on Anne's shoulder. She gently placed his head back in position and scrunched closer to the window away from her dead companion. She glanced at her watch. Six more hours until they landed. But only a half hour until dinner.

Chapter Two

The plane jerked its way onto the runway at O'Hare Airport before sliding to a stop, startling Anne and waking her up. She clutched the armrests on either side. She reached under her seat to make sure her large orange Prada bag didn't fly into the aisle. She hoped Bernie wouldn't either. She could hear the high-pitched yapping of a dog back in coach. She hoped it wasn't near CC.

As the plane taxied to the gate, the captain announced, "Please remain seated until the fasten your seat belt light is off. We have a medical emergency." Before the captain could finish, the door flew open. Two EMTs wheeling a gurney down the narrow aisle, made their way to Anne's row. A short while later, the gurney made its journey back off the plane, its passenger covered by a white sheet. An arm popped out from underneath the sheet. Bernie's Timex was still ticking but he wasn't. Bernie had taken his last flight.

Anne waited her turn to disembark, following behind the other first class passengers. Betsy had gotten off first, waving her three fingers at Anne and blowing her air kisses. "Buttersworth," Anne muttered. The truce had ended. They were back on American soil, and their amnesty didn't cross international lines.

On her way out, Anne stopped to talk to the flight attendant, "Do you know what happened to Bernie?"

"I'm not allowed to talk about it. Airline regulations," the attendant said.

Anne stepped off the plane and stood in the waiting area, watching the wrinkled coach passengers file off. She had yet to see CC. Tapping her foot, she decided she couldn't wait any longer and thought it a good idea to check out the duty-free shops. Bernie's passing had upset her but she felt he'd understand if she moved on. They'd only known each other a short while, and it wasn't as though she could help him. Shopping was the only cure to make her feel normal again. What a sad conclusion to a beautiful trip.

O'Hare International Terminal Five had some great stores like Armani, Michael Kors and her favorite, Ferragamo. Who didn't love an Italian shoe? She'd start there. By the time CC found her, open shoeboxes and a hovering salesman surrounded her. "Anne, really?" CC asked. "Didn't you do enough shopping? We're not going to have room for everything in the car."

"CC, I'm distraught. It was a very traumatic flight. Six hours next to a dead body and you'd be shopping, too," Anne said. "Besides, look at these, CC, they're peau de soie." Anne admired the brown pumps in the mirror, twisting her foot in every direction. "I think I'll take them." Anne sat down, took the pumps off and handed them to the salesman.

"Very well." He put them into the box and closed the lid. He moved toward the register.

"Wait, I'll take those, too." Anne pointed at the pink satin sandals. "Aren't these perfect for a summer afternoon picnic?" She asked CC.

"If you're a five-year-old," CC replied.

"Oh, and these too," Anne picked up another box from the pile. She handed the salesman her debit card.

The salesman ran her card and frowned. "It says your card has been declined."

"Declined?" Anne repeated. "That's not possible. Run it again."

He swiped the card again. "It says *declined*. Call your bank." He handed the card back to Anne. "Do you have another form of payment?"

"I don't understand." Anne held up her finger. "Let me call my bank." She stepped away from the register and called from her cell phone. She explained the situation to the bank representative.

"Miss Hillstrom, you show a negative balance of $12,000 in your checking account."

"What? How can that be?" Anne shouted into the phone. "My checking account is linked to my savings account. The last time I checked I had plenty of money in my savings account."

"I see that you've made a lot of purchases recently. The last purchase you made for $12,000 brought your account into the negative."

"I had over a $100,000 when I left Paris a couple hours ago," Anne said.

"There's been over a $100,000 in purchases in the last couple hours. Because of your buying history and because all the purchases except for one were made in France, the purchases didn't set any fraud alarms off."

"Yes, yes. I know I've done a lot of shopping recently but not in the past few hours, I was on a plane. I didn't make those purchases." Anne stopped. "What was the last purchase for $12,000?"

"It was South Seas Jewelry in Singapore, and it was a point of sale purchase."

"That's impossible. I've never even been to Singapore."

"In that case, someone stole your identity, and we'll open an investigation."

The shoe salesman watched Anne as her jaw dropped open. He couldn't hear what she was saying but the fear in her eyes was apparent. Something was wrong, very very wrong.

Anne staggered for a moment and then dropped back on the bench. "That wasn't me," she repeated.

"We'll start an investigation."

"Yes, yes," Anne stammered. "My friend is a Chicago police detective—Nigel Towers, very tall and very British. He can help." Anne became more frantic, her breathing grew rapid, coming in and out in short gasps.

CC came up to her. "Anne, what's wrong?"

Anne was hyperventilating. CC put both her hands on her shoulders and looked her in the eyes. She was floating away from reality. CC pulled her back. "Anne, just breathe."

"CC. Money. Gone." Anne gasped out.

CC sat down next to her, put her arm around her and slowly took the phone out of her hand. CC spoke into it, "Who is this? What's going on here?"

The bank representative replied, "I'm sorry. Who is this?"

"CC Muller. Who is this?"

"I'm Sarah Kundson with Chase Bank."

"What's going on?" CC asked.

"I'm sorry. I can't give you any of Miss Hillstrom's personal information without her approval."

CC stuck the phone by Anne's face. "Anne, tell her it's okay for me to talk to her."

"CC good," Anne gasped out in between her deep breaths. She was counting to ten in her head but had lost count and needed to start over. None of her relaxation methods were working.

"What's going on with Anne's account?" CC asked.

"She has an overdraft of $12,000 and a zero balance in her savings account."

"How can that be?" CC asked.

The woman recounted what she had told Anne and gave CC the case number for the investigation she had just opened. CC hung up and sat back down next to Anne. "CC, did she tell you? $12,000? I had much more than that in my account not more than two weeks ago. I know I spent some in Paris."

"Some?" CC interrupted.

"All right," Anne conceded. "A lot of money, but not all of it."

"Somebody stole your identity. You know, Anne, you were throwing your card around everywhere in Paris. When's the last time you used it before we got on the flight?"

Anne thought for a moment. "I bought a couple magazines for the plane, a book, some snacks. Oh, I forgot, I bought this." She flipped the collar of her dress revealing the flora and fauna Cartier diamond, emerald and ruby brooch. "It was on sale. I remember now the sales clerk was having a hard time swiping my card. She had to read my number out over the phone to authorize it. She was speaking in French so I couldn't understand her."

CC sighed. "Anne, really? In a crowded airport gift shop."

Anne interrupted, "Cartier."

"She was reading your personal information out loud over a phone."

"Like I said, CC, it was in French. I don't know what she was saying. It sounded like numbers."

"Let's head home. We can figure things out from there," CC said, putting her arm around her friend's shoulder.

Anne gave a parting glance at the shoes and followed CC to customs. There was a line waiting to clear. She balanced her bag on her shoulder and kept a tight hold on the vintage Louis Vuitton rolling bag she had found at a Paris flea market. She tapped her foot impatiently while she stood in line. "Seriously, can't they open another lane?" Anne stared at the four empty counters. Only two counters were open. A customs agent walked past Anne. "Excuse me, excuse me," she said.

The young man turned to Anne.

"Is this going to be much longer? Can't you open up another counter? I only have these two bags. After all, we're coming from Paris. I was flying first class, and it's not like it's Istanbul."

The young man looked over Anne with a careful eye. "Ma'am, there's heightened security. We need to check all carry-ons thoroughly and that's slowing up the line."

"Last time I traveled internationally all I had to do to get back in the country was fill out a yellow card."

"How long ago was that?"

"At least 15 years ago," Anne replied.

The young man smiled. "Things have changed a bit." He walked away.

Anne tapped CC on her shoulder. She took her earbuds out. "Anne, what do you want?"

"The customs agent. Did you hear what he was saying?"

CC whispered, "They're looking for someone."

"What are you talking about?"

"I was listening to the police band."

"Are those even legal anymore?"

"Journalist." CC put her earbuds back in and turned back toward the front of the line. Anne watched as each carry-on was painstakingly searched and frowned at some of the cheap items like the imitation Chanel bag. She could tell from 50 feet away, it was a knockoff. She could also smell the overpowering dime store fragrance. At least she was confident that all they would find in her bags was original vintage scarves, brass candlesticks and jet jewelry. She smiled at herself.

Anne thought, *money doesn't buy happiness but it's a good start.*

It was finally her turn. She lifted her bag onto the stainless steel table and slowly unzipped it. The young woman searching through the bag, pulled out her Hermes scarf and dumped it on the table. Anne snatched it up. "That's Hermes."

The woman said, "You have to put it back. You're not allowed to touch anything."

One precious item after another was pulled from her bag with no regard to its beauty or its price tag. Anne watched quietly, breathing deep, counting to ten, her lips moving as she counted. She noticed three other agents standing to the side talking. Her eyes locked on the bag of Garrett's popcorn that one of the agents was eating. The smell of caramel corn and cheese lofted over, filling her senses.

"Ma'am, ma'am, we're done. You can leave now," the agent said.

"Chicago style," Anne said out loud.

"What was that?" the agent asked.

"Nothing," Anne said, turning back to face the agent.

The agent zipped her bag shut, stamped her passport and handed it back to her.

Anne joined CC on the other side of customs. They were officially back on U.S. soil. "CC, can we please stop at terminal one?"

"Why?"

"Garrett's popcorn."

"We can't get to it from here. You have to go back through security."

Anne thought about purchasing a ticket to get to the terminal then she remembered she was broke. She followed CC out to the street and waited for the shuttle. It dropped them off at long-term parking where CC's beloved 1968 VW bus was parked. A heavy snow was falling. The Chicago wind whipped around them. The bus was covered with an inch of fresh snow. CC brushed the snow from the windows, using the sleeve of her coat. They piled into the car. The engine started right up as CC knew it would. She strained to look out the frosted window as she pulled out of the parking space. Heading home, never seeing the man watching them.

Chapter Three

After putting her bags inside her crowded kitchen, Anne walked the short distance to her next-door neighbor and cat sitter, Grandma Jan Kustodia. Grandma Jan, the neighborhood watch, the woman everyone went to when they needed something, anything. Anne climbed the back stairs that led to Grandma Jan's apartment above her daughter's house. She stood looking out into the yard, which was immaculate. All the leaves had been raked, the sidewalk shoveled. She glanced over into her yard, which showed traces of brown leaves underneath the white snow. She had left in such a hurry she never prepared her backyard for winter. She knew if she didn't take care of it quickly, Grandma Jan would be over with a shovel and a rake. Jan had a low tolerance for untidy situations. Anne knocked on the door, pulling the collar of her new North Face jacket around her neck.

"Coming," Anne heard the familiar voice of her dear friend. The door opened. Grandma Jan was holding a steaming mug of what Anne knew was Jewel Eight O'Clock Extra Bold coffee, Jan's drink of choice. "Oh, Anne, you're home. How are you, dear?" Jan held the screen door open wide enough so Anne could step inside. Then she hugged her.

"I just got home."

"Did you have a wonderful time, dear? I did see some of your postings on the blog."

"It was a wonderful trip. Many great finds. Paris is lovely at this time of year. And, oh, the food. The croissants, the bread."

Jan took a step back and looked Anne over. She did the calculation in her head. Twelve, fourteen pounds as she took her jacket off revealing the Chanel silk blouse straining at the buttons. "Sit down, sit down, dear. I'll make you a cup of coffee."

"That's okay. It was a long flight. I want to pick up Sassy, go home and take a nap."

Grandma Jan became concerned. "Anne, dear, sit down for a moment."

Anne squeezed in behind the little breakfast bench. "Jan, you're making me nervous. Did something happen to Sassy? Is she okay?"

"I'm so sorry. Yes, dear," she said with a nervous laugh. "She's perfectly healthy for a cat in her condition."

"Condition? Now I'm really worried. What condition?"

"Come take a look." Jan led the way into her small guest bedroom where Sassy lay like the queen she was on the guest bed. She lifted her head slowly and blinked with recognition at Anne. Anne ran to her, petting her soft fur, hugging her.

"Sassy, you look horrible. You've gained so much weight."

Jan bit her tongue, not wanting to tell Anne she had done the same. Anne turned to Jan with tears in her eyes. "She's pregnant," Jan said. "She's okay. She's going to have kittens. Sassy's going to be a momma."

"What? How?"

"The usual how. Obviously you never had Sassy spayed."

'She was supposed to be a housecat."

"She spends more time out of the house than in the house."

"Are you sure she's expecting?"

"I had Dr. Brian come check her. She was throwing up a lot and it turns out it was morning sickness. Brian confirmed she's perfectly healthy. She will have a normal delivery."

"We'll take good care of you and your babies, Sassy," Anne said. Sassy lay her head down, closing her blue eyes. Anne wondered where she would put kittens in her already overflowing house. There would have to be new tree houses, scratching posts, litter boxes. Her head began to spin as she contemplated all the valuables she would have to put away. It meant a fourth storage unit for sure. And, then there'd be the added expense.

"Why don't we let her sleep?" Jan asked. "You go home and take a nap. We can talk about it more later. I'm sure you have lots of unpacking to do."

"Okay, Jan." Anne stood up. "By the way, I almost forgot. I got you a little thank you gift for watching Sassy."

"You didn't have to do that," Jan said.

Anne reached into her bag and pulled out a beautiful gold enamel pendant. It had an image of a woman with flowing long hair carved into it. "This is a French Limoges painted enamel pendant from the Victorian era. I found it in a little antique shop near the Seine. The shop has quite a history, dating all the way back to Napoleon days. Next door, by the way, is a little café that serves the most scrumptious crepes." Anne could picture them in her mind, drizzling with butter and whipped cream. She broke her trance. "CC was able to procure the recipe from the chef. I'll have her make you some."

Outside, they could hear the beeping of a truck backing up. "What is that?" Jan asked.

"They're here!" Anne exclaimed, leaping off the bed, running to the front window. Three semis were pulling up in front of Anne's bungalow next door.

"What's here?" Jan asked, peeking out the curtains next to her. "Anne, are you moving?"

"No, of course not. It's souvenirs from my trip."

"All that?"

Anne didn't answer. She flew out the door, heading to the front of the house to supervise the unloading of the containers. Jan grabbed her jacket and followed behind her. Anne instructed the first driver to back into her driveway, all the way to her two-car detached garage located on the back of her lot.

"What are you going to do with three semis full of souvenirs? You have no room in your garage," Jan asked, standing and staring.

"I bought the containers. I'm going to park them in the driveway for now."

"There's no way they're going to fit."

"It's just temporary. I'm going to clear out my garage and unload them into it."

Anne got into her Mercury Mystique, which was packed as full as the shipping containers. Grandma Jan watched as she moved the car onto Linden Avenue. When the men were done, Anne was able to park two of the containers onto her long driveway. The third container ended up on the street in front of her house. Even though she disapproved, Grandma Jan supervised the landing operation.

"I think you're right. I'm really tired. I'll leave Sassy with you if you don't mind," Anne said.

Jan placed her hands on her hips, looked over the containers in the driveway and then at the one on the street. "Anne, sweetheart, this can't stay on the street. You're going to be fined."

"It's just temporary." Anne gave Grandma Jan a hug and headed into her house. From her vantage point on the sidewalk, Grandma Jan stood in the wake, shaking her head. At the end of the block, the man in the dark sedan watched.

Chapter Four

CC flipped the crepes on the pan, humming softly to herself. The chef at the little French café had taught her the trick to flipping crepes. It was too late in the season for fresh blueberries but not for her preserves. She'd put up bushels full. She went into the basement to the section she called her root cellar and retrieved a jar. On her heels was Bandit, her Australian shepherd, who hadn't left her side since she arrived home from Paris. She'd picked him up from her brother's house before returning home. Bandit watched carefully as CC warmed the blueberry preserves. When she was done, she put some in the middle of the crepe and folded it in a square, the French way. She topped it with a large dollop of fresh whipped cream. "Voila," she said with a French flair. She took out the French press she'd bought at the Parisian market and then she prepared the coffee.

She peeked out the bay window above her double country sink. Almost a full acre of land; she hadn't prepared for winter yet with her sudden trip. There would be pruning and mulching and preparing the koi pond for the winter. Then there was her work for the steel magazine. She hadn't filed a story in two months after getting caught up in Anne's whirlwind of traveling and shopping windfall. And, then there was the Spoon Sisters blog. With the success of the blog, she neither had the time or the financial need to write for the magazine. Even though she did love steel. She picked up the stainless steel spatula and prepared the crepes for plating as she heard a knock at the door. Bandit jumped to attention, barking his high-pitched bark. Anne walked in, carrying her large orange Prada bag.

"CC, it's me," she said from the hallway.

"Come in, Anne, breakfast is almost ready."

"That's great. I'm starving. I've been sorting through the containers all morning."

CC turned around to look at her old friend. "Containers? There's more than one?"

"There's a couple," Anne said.

"Couple like two?"

"More like three."

CC turned off the stove and walked into the living room. "Three semi containers full of stuff?"

"It's not stuff. And some of it's for our fans." Anne pulled a binder out of her bag. "That's our agenda for this morning—to contact our fans and place these orphaned artifacts."

"Hmmph," CC said. "Sit down. Breakfast is ready. We'll talk about it over crepes."

"Yummy, I thought I smelled crepes when I walked in. Is this Chef Pierre's recipe?"

"Yes, with a little secret ingredient," CC said placing the plates on the table.

Anne frowned. CC was renowned for her hot pepper patch. She'd been known to say more than once that hot peppers make everything better. Anne sat at the mid-century modern table. She had offered to buy CC a dining room set in France, a lovely Louis XIV gold and gilt-leafed ornate rectangular table with matching hand-stitched fleur de lis brocade chairs. CC preferred the modern clean practical lines of her teak set so Anne had bought the set for herself, unable to resist it. It was now sitting in container number three. She cautiously bit into the crepe, tasting the sweet blueberries, waiting for the bite of a ghost pepper.

"I did not put any peppers in these. I would never put peppers in a crepe," CC said, sipping her coffee.

Anne poured an enormous amount of cream into her coffee and added four sugar cubes. CC gave her a disapproving look. "Now that we're back home, we have to talk about your diet."

"What diet?" Anne asked, looking up with a dab of whipped cream on her lip.

"That's my point," CC said. "Vacation's over. It's time to get back to work, which includes cutting back a bit. Speaking of work, when are you going back to work?"

Anne didn't answer, finishing her third crepe. She stared down at her plate, avoiding CC's glance. "I kind of might have given my two-week notice before we left for Paris. It actually was like a two-day notice."

"Anne, how could you?"

"CC, I had enough money, job-quitting money. Besides, the blog is my full-time job."

"Anne, how could you?" CC repeated. "What are you going to do now? You have no money."

"Something will turn up. I talked to the bank. They're investigating the identity theft."

"That can take months. What will you live on?"

"Funny you should ask. I was going through the papers this morning and found several estate sales, an auction in Chicago. I've mapped out an itinerary for today. I thought we could do some flips, some quick buys and sell on eBay."

"What about the list you have already? Aren't the items in the three containers you have for our fans?"

Anne hesitated. "I'm not sure yet. I'm still deciding what I'm ready to part with. That's going to take some time."

"You need to get rid of those containers quickly. You have to liquidate and get some cash."

"You mean like a yard sale? How can I make money on a French bouillotte lamp? I paid $800 for the French empire style and $1,000 for a 34-inch brass Chapman. Can you imagine a yard sale? Oh, I'll give you a $1.50 for the Chapman if you carry it to my car. Or, offering me 50 cents for my Chanel earrings that I paid over $1,500 for? This walnut Louis XV needlepoint Bergere armchair is quite comfortable, would you take $5 for it?"

"I was thinking more like we should have a pop-up antique sale. Something temporary so you can earn some fast cash."

Anne put her fork down as her face turned white. Her lips moved but nothing came out.

"Anne, breathe." CC put her hand on her friend's arm. "It's going to be okay. We'll do this together. I'm taking a leave of absence from the magazine and here's what we're going to do. We're going to reach out to our blog list fans with their requested items. Your other finds we will sell. Only the ones that you can absolutely live without."

Anne mouthed, "Live without?"

"My ex has a little frame house he's been rehabbing for eight years in downtown Glen Ellyn. It's between the Sweet Shop and Pete's Pizza. It's the perfect location for a pop-up antique sale. I'm sure I can talk him into letting us use it for the sale. We'll put the word out on the blog which is now at almost a hundred thousand fans and you'll have your money back in no time."

"Live without?" Anne whispered.

After finishing breakfast, they walked to downtown Glen Ellyn. Bandit sniffed every corner. The cold air was refreshing, typical of an Illinois winter. They reached the little block of stores in the quaint four-square block shopping section. Amongst the gourmet popcorn store, children's toy store, and the grill, there it stood, the nearly hundred-year-old blue wood-frame two-story. The stairs and front porch falling apart, one window boarded over. "How long has your ex been working on this house?" Anne asked CC.

"I'm sure it looks better on the inside." They walked up the two stairs onto the squeaking front porch. They peeked inside the non-boarded over window. Insulation lay over the floor along with broken beer bottles. Some water damage on the back wall exposed the studs. Overall, a testament to CC's ex-husband's work ethic.

"Really, CC, this is where you want me to put my velvet fainting couch?"

"Anne, a couple days cleaning up, some patching the walls, it'll be as good as new."

Anne sighed, staring across the street at the gourmet popcorn store. "My diet starts tomorrow." She reached inside her large orange Prada bag and opened her Bottega Venetta change purse. She counted quarters and nickels.

"Oh, Anne, I've got this," CC said. After getting their popcorn, they headed back to CC's house.

After Anne left, CC pulled out her MacBook and opened up her blog site. "Dear friends, I have exciting news. Anne and I have a surplus of antiques, so much so that we've decided to host a Spoon Sisters pop-up antique sale. We've found the perfect location in downtown Glen Ellyn, a short drive west of Chicago. More details will follow as we grow closer to the date but I wanted you, our loyal fans, to be the first to know." As she was writing, she perused the list of requests from their avid readers. She recognized one name immediately, Professor Gildwin. He was the fan who'd told Anne about the sale at the art school in Paris.

She opened his email. "Dear CC, I see from your last blog that the art school sale was a success. I am most interested in the drawing table. It would be perfect for my study. Please let me know how I might purchase it. Sincerely, Professor Edwin Gildwin."

CC remembered that drawing desk. She actually had wanted it for her art studio but with Anne in dire straits she'd have to let it go. She would wait to answer him until she talked to Anne.

After posting the blog, she scanned her long list of emails, both work related and personal. She hadn't kept on top of them when they were in Paris. She opened one from her cousin who lived in Munich, Germany. She asked if her daughter could stay with CC while she studied journalism at Columbia College. CC beamed; she relished the thought of being a mentor to her young cousin. CC quickly replied, "Of course, I haven't seen Ingrid in years. I'd love to see her, and she is most welcome. I have plenty of room."

Chapter Five

CC turned onto Anne's street. Not finding space in front of the house, she parked down the block. Walking up the long driveway, she squeezed past the containers that pushed over onto the grass. CC could hear clattering noises coming from the garage and Anne yelling. When she reached the garage entrance, she made out the top of Anne's head all the way in the back of the garage, popping up and down occasionally like a creature in a Whack-A-Mole game. "Anne, what are you doing?"

The mole's head popped up. "Making room!" she screamed, balancing a Chinese armchair on top of a mahogany curved curio cabinet.

CC gazed around the garage, which was stacked to the ceiling with Anne's treasures curated from years of hunting and gathering. She didn't know how Anne would make it out alive. In fact, she didn't know how Anne had made it into the garage. "Anne, come out now, we have to talk."

Anne climbed over the top of a Waterfall dresser, sliding over like a seal, landing at CC's feet. "I'm still working on the first container but I put a dent in it. I think I can make room for everything."

CC looked at the open container behind her. "I talked to my ex. He said we could use the house for the sale."

Anne's breathing became shallow, her face turned white. She couldn't speak.

"I've already gotten back several hundred replies about the sale. It's going to be a full house, and I've applied for permits from the city. Because it's zoned commercial, the city requires us to apply for insurance coverage."

Anne bent over trying to catch her breath. She reached up and closed the overhead garage door before walking into the open container. She retrieved a large ormolu vase. "My precious." She cradled it in her arms. She walked up to the house. CC followed behind. She was worried that her old friend was losing it. Not that that was a far journey for Anne, but between the identity theft and the thought of selling all her antiques, Anne was teetering on the edge. CC followed her through the back door and into the kitchen. She sat at the table as Anne carefully placed the vase on the floor next to a stack of yellow envelopes. "CC, would you like some tea?"

"Sure, Anne, that would be lovely."

Anne grabbed her favorite teapot, the one her Great Aunt Sybil had given her. The one that was once owned by Sir Arthur Conan Doyle. She filled it with water and put it on the stove. She sat next to CC. "I don't think I can do it," she said. "I don't think I can part with any of it. The money's gone, the trip's over. This is all I have left to show for it."

CC's glance turned to the yellow envelopes. "Anne, what are those?"

"Nothing, just fines from the city. They're not happy about the containers. Apparently I have 30 days to get rid of the containers or the fines will double. There's a new ticket on the container every day."

"Then we have to move this along. You don't have a choice. Tomorrow, we'll start cleaning the house," CC said.

Anne brought over two steaming cups of tea. She went into her empty fridge and then into the pantry. She pulled out an old box of Nilla wafers. She placed them on a Flora Danica plate she'd bought at the Lake Forest church rummage sale. CC looked at the plate. "Anne, I thought you'd sold these to the person on the list?"

"I might have kept one for myself." Anne didn't mention that the plate's match was in her pantry.

CC frowned but didn't respond. "I received an email from my cousin in Munich. Her daughter is coming to study journalism at Columbia College and will be staying with me."

"For the semester?"

"I'm not sure how long but she's flying in next week."

"That's great. It's Ingrid, right? I remember I met her at your Christmas party years ago. This is exciting."

They sipped their tea. A loud crash interrupted their conversation. "What was that?" Anne jumped up and flew out the door, heading towards the garage. The garage door was partially open, a chair leg sticking out from underneath. Anne pushed the door open. The Chinese dragon chair had toppled off its perch. It was mortally wounded, one leg split in two. She glanced at CC. "How did the door open? It couldn't open by itself."

The roar of a plane flying overhead, muffled the sound of the car speeding off in the distance.

Chapter Six

"Are you sure this is a good idea?" Anne asked as she followed CC into the two-story building.

"My ex said we could use it. It's a perfect location." CC opened the door. The first thing that greeted them was the smell. A combination of musk, wet plaster and cigarettes. The second thing to greet them was the realization that it would take a lot of work to clean the space. Empty fast food containers, rusty tools littered the floor.

"It looks like squatters settled in," Anne said.

CC put down her broom, put her hands on her hips and looked around. "Nope, just him." She pushed up her sleeves and opened a garbage bag. "Let's clean."

Anne cracked open a window, one of the few windows without broken glass. The sweet shop next door was making caramels, the smell of brown sugar and butter wafted over Anne, lifting her a foot off the ground. By lunchtime, they had cleared all the rubble and debris out. A good start to a good idea. As they walked out onto the front porch, a large angry woman wearing an apron that read Sweet Shop, covered in caramel stood waiting for them, arms crossed. "It's about time," the woman said.

"Time for what?"

"That this eyesore was taken care of. I've been complaining to the village for years now."

"It's only temporary," Anne said.

"What do you mean, temporary?"

"This is exciting. We're having a pop-up antique sale."

"Pop-up? What's that?"

"It's a limited time only sale. Don't worry. We won't be here long," CC explained.

"So, what you're telling me is that you're going to have a bunch of people taking up my parking spots, making a mess and then you're going to leave and this dump is going back to how it was?"

Anne nodded. "Exactly."

"Shhh, Anne." CC turned and hushed Anne. "It'll be good for your business. I'm sure a lot of our fans will stop at your store."

"Fans? Are you celebrities?"

"Kind of. Spoon Sisters." Anne pointed first to CC then to herself then back to CC then back to herself.

"Funny, you two don't look like sisters."

"We're not sisters, we're partners."

"I have no problem with that lifestyle but I still don't want any trouble from you two." She turned on her heel and walked away.

"What does she mean by lifestyle?" Anne asked.

"Don't mind her. Let's go get a salad," CC said.

Anne looked to the left, saw the pizza place, looked across the street at the fried chicken shack. Then she followed CC down the block to the organic kitchen. As they sat eating their kale and blueberry salads, CC said, "Anne, I wanted to ask you. I've had some inquiries about items from the fan list. Items I posted pictures of. That we bought in Paris. People want to know when they can pay for them and when we can send them out."

Anne put her fork down. "I'm still sorting through everything. I'm halfway through the second container."

"We can start by getting rid of the drawing desk. The professor who told us about the sale at the art school would like it. He'll even come out to pick it up."

Not speaking, Anne picked out the blueberries from her salad, leaving the kale behind.

"Anne, the drawing desk?" CC asked.

"I'm not sure I'm ready to part with it," Anne said. She didn't want to say that she was thinking of refurbishing it and giving it to CC for either her or Ingrid.

"What are you going to do with it?"

"I'm not sure yet."

They finished their meal and went back to the shop. At the end of the day, they stood and surveyed the efforts of their hard work. The original wood floors gleamed after a bucket of Murphy's oil soap. The one stained glass dining room window remained intact. The other three windows were replaced with new glass and putty. CC had become quite the handywoman. "Not too bad," CC said. "A little fresh paint and we're in business."

"This is just temporary, right?"

"Of course, but we have to make it presentable. We have a reputation."

"What's next?"

"We get together this weekend to take pictures of what we're going to include in the sale. In the meantime, you can research prices and tag items. My ex said we can use his pickup to bring over the larger furniture items."

"I'm exhausted. Can we call it a day?"

"Should we meet up tomorrow to review the plans?" CC asked.

"Can we meet later? I have some things I want to do in the morning," Anne said.

"What are you doing?"

"I wanted to stop at Goodwill, Savers and a few estate sales."

"And how are you going to pay for that?"

"Oh, yeah, I forgot. But it is an investment; I can look for things to resell."

"I'll meet you here at one o'clock."

Anne walked the few blocks to her Mercury Mystique. It was filled to the brim but she was too tired to stop at the storage locker. She would only be able to pick up small items tomorrow. She pulled onto the curb next to her house. It was getting dark but she could see the fluorescent yellow paper sticking out of her front door. Another ticket, she sighed. She hadn't paid the first tickets yet. She went to examine the containers, trying to figure out how to squeeze all three in the driveway. That's when she noticed, the first padlock broken off. She ran to the second container, its padlock was broken. And, then the third container, the same. Her heart pounded, the fear rising in her. She opened the container door. From what she could see, nothing was missing. She immediately hit her speed dial. From the other end of the phone, the very British sounding Nigel Towers answered, "Anne, so lovely to hear from you. Are you back home?"

"I've been home for a while."

"Oh, right. How was your trip?"

"Nigel, we don't have time for that. We have an emergency."

"Anne, are you okay?"

"I can't talk about it on the phone. Can you please come over?"

"Anne, I'm on my way." Nigel hung up.

Anne stared at the phone in her hand for a moment before entering the container. She moved things around to see if anything was missing. It was hard in the dim light to tell. From the bushes, a pair of red eyes glowed watching, always watching. Anne could feel the piercing stare. A shiver ran down her neck. She glanced again, only to see a tuft of fluffy white fur weaving in and out of the pine trees. "Sassy, what are you doing out here? What mischief have you been up to? You should be in the house resting. You have to think of the babies." Anne picked up the Persian, carrying her to the back door. She deposited the cat in the kitchen as Nigel pulled up in his unmarked Chevy Caprice.

Anne watched as he ducked his head down, his chin almost touching his spindly knees as he unfolded himself out of the vehicle. No matter what was going on in Anne's life, seeing Nigel was good. "Nigel," Anne said, giving him an awkward hug. "What's with the beard?"

Nigel instinctively rubbed the whiskers on his chin. "Just a bit of fun. I thought it was time I changed things up a bit."

Anne noticed Nigel was wearing the paisley flowered tie she'd given him. She'd found it at an estate sale. Nigel always remembered the small things that made Anne smile. She thought the beard was a good addition. It made him look a little more rugged. "Anne, what's the problem?"

"Come, look, it's terrifying." She led him to the containers.

Nigel examined the broken padlocks. "Was anything taken?"

"Not that I can tell."

"What is all this anyway?" He stared at the three containers.

"Souvenirs from my trip."

"Were they out of the Eiffel Tower miniatures?"

"Oh, no, I bought those, too. I even bought you one."

"Aces."

Looking him over, she noticed his suit. "Is that new?"

"Yes," he said, puffing himself up. His bony shoulders stuck out through the Italian merino wool.

"You look very nice, Nigel."

"Thank you."

"Are you working? Do you want to come in for tea?"

"Actually, I was on my way somewhere."

"For work?"

"No."

"Oh." Anne's face fell.

"I actually have a date."

"Oh, a date, that's wonderful. So sorry I bothered you."

"Oh, no bother. This is serious business. Someone trying to break into your souvenir containers. I'll send a uniformed officer here to make a report."

She reached in her purse and pulled out ten yellow envelopes. "Is there anything you can do about these fines? I'm working on moving the containers."

"It's not really my jurisdiction. I can make some phone calls. I think it's best you move the containers."

"We're working on that. CC and I are having a pop-up antique sale."

"What a brilliant idea!"

"Yes, we're fixing up a little two-story frame house in downtown Glen Ellyn. CC's ex owns it and said we could borrow it."

"Oh, brilliant. Let me know when; I'd love to come."

"You're definitely invited."

He looked at his watch. "Do you want me to stay with you until the uniform comes? We can run to the hardware store to get some good padlocks."

"Oh, no, you have a date. You have to go."

"It was nice seeing you."

Nigel stood awkwardly, bending over Anne looking like a question mark. Anne wondered what the question was. She wanted desperately to give him a kiss but resisted the urge. She'd given up that right. "Okay, then, thank you, Nigel. Have fun." Anne smiled and then went into the house. As Nigel drove off into the night and his new life, Anne retrieved three padlocks from the box of 40 she'd bought at a yard sale. She locked up the containers for the night, then she took a cautious step about the street. She was tired and scared. Not for herself but for her containers. She had thought she could talk CC out of selling everything but now she knew it had to be done.

Chapter Seven

Saturday morning, Anne put the teakettle on. She was wrapped up in her flannel robe. She was freezing. She went over and checked the thermostat. It said 55. She tapped on it again and turned it up to 80. She waited for the familiar knocking of the old Carrier furnace. Nothing happened. She tapped on the thermostat again. She went to check on the tea. The kettle was ice cold. She lifted up the kettle to check the flame. There was none.

She grabbed a Diet Coke from the fridge and an oversized chocolate muffin from Costco. She sat down at the kitchen table. Sassy leaped up, trying to take her perch above the table on the oak shelf. She couldn't make it. Instead she settled down on a chair next to Anne who stroked her soft white fur. "Sassy, you're going to have to take it easy," Anne said.

Anne sifted through the piles of envelopes that had gathered over the past few weeks until she reached several from Nicor Gas. She ripped them open—first, second, third and final notice. Then she put them down. "Oh, dear."

Sassy perked her head up. "Nothing for you to worry about, Sassy." Anne quickly got dressed and went out to her containers. She pulled out each treasure into the driveway, giving it a look over, saying her goodbyes. Sassy watched from the kitchen window, nodding approvingly. There would be little mouths to feed. Anne would have to sacrifice.

As she reached the back of the first container, she found the drawing desk that CC had mentioned. She could make a quick flip, enough to pay the gas bill. She admired the French oak practical lines of the desk. It was perfect for CC. What a great Christmas present it would make. She dragged it carefully toward the garage so it would be out of CC's view. She opened the garage door and wedged the desk in between her grandfather's bedroom set and her childhood baby carriage. She thought about her Great Aunt Sybil, her antique mentor, and what she would say about selling all these beautiful finds. Anne had scoured antique stores, flea markets and boutiques throughout Paris and beyond. She walked back to the first container and grabbed the Louis XVI desk chair. She placed it carefully in the garage. She thought about the hours, the days she'd spent walking along the cobblestone sidewalks, her feet aching. She went to the second container and grabbed the 18th century gold gilt mirror. She made room for it in the garage. Aunt Sybil would say that every lost treasure deserves a good home, that the pieces speak to you, they choose their owners, not the other way around. Anne understood that, she had that same passion as Great Aunt Sybil, that need to give a good home to orphaned artifacts. She went back to the driveway and continued saving her selection of orphaned artifacts, occasionally scanning the street to check for CC. Maybe it was her countless hours spent playing Tetris or her determination but she made an entire container's worth of souvenirs fit in an already overstuffed garage. She hurriedly closed the garage door as she heard the pickup truck, the big F-250 diesel, pull up the street. CC had borrowed it from her ex.

CC got out and went to the first container. "That's a new padlock," CC said.

"I had to change them out. Somebody tried breaking in."

"What are you talking about?"

"When I got home yesterday, the locks were broken but nothing was missing. Nigel thought it could have been neighborhood kids."

"Nigel?"

"Yes, of course. I called Nigel when I saw the locks broken."

"Anne, he's a Chicago detective. Why would he come out to the burbs?"

"He looked really nice. He grew a beard. Actually quite handsome."

"I thought you two were just friends now."

"We are. He was on his way to a date."

"Oh. How do you feel about that?"

"I'm fine. It was my idea to just be friends. He wanted more but I'm not ready for that commitment." Anne turned her attention back to the containers and opened the first one.

"Anne, I thought this was a lot fuller before," CC said.

"Nope, nope, that's about right."

Anne helped CC load the first few items onto the pickup. After the first trip, Anne surveyed the contents of her containers on the store floor. It looked better with her belongings inside, and the little frame house was nice and warm. *Actually*, she thought, *her vintage fainting couch might be a good place to take a nap*. She laid down and closed her eyes while CC continued carrying in furniture. "Anne, what are you doing?"

"I was testing the couch. If we're going to sell it, I want to make sure it's in good condition." Anne sat up.

"Better condition than you're in," CC muttered as she went back outside.

As CC emptied the truck, Anne moved furniture around, placing them in groupings. The small store was getting quite full. It reminded her of her living room. CC brought in the last bookcase. "I don't think we can fit another load in here." She surveyed the room.

"You have to move your truck. I've got a delivery coming," the woman from the sweet shop said, standing in the doorway, hands on hips.

"By the way, I'm CC and this is Anne."

"Yes, I know, you're partners."

"And you are?"

"I'm getting tired of waiting for you to move your truck." The sweet shop lady backed up and left.

"Not a problem. I'll do that right now." CC grabbed the keys out of her pocket.

Chapter Eight

CC plunged the sign into the ground outside of the two-story building. "This is it," she said, turning to Anne. The sign read, "Sale, This Weekend Only." Anne saw the sweet shop lady next door peeking out her window, grimacing. She thought, *How could someone who works with sweets all day be so sour?*

"Let's go open the shop." CC led the way up the front stairs. On the front porch sat a milk pail full of dry flowers from CC's garden, a rocking chair and various garden pots. A wreath made of black maple leaves and birch branches decorated the front door. Inside Anne had arranged all the items she could part with, that CC was aware of, by era, style and circumstance.

A butcher-block counter with an old-fashioned cash register was located in the front of the store. In the back room, the old Hotpoint stove fired up. CC steamed milk to make hot chocolate. Anne wandered around the store, turning on lights and making sure everything was just right. She checked all the price tags to make sure they were facing up so customers could see them, one of her pet peeves.

The tag dangling from a 1930 Eastlake mirror read, *$100*. Anne looked to the left and then to the right. She pulled a pen out of her pocket, crossed out the *$100* and wrote *$200*. Standing in the corner was a bi-fold display of original barbershop illustrations with ten 8 x 10 portraits taken by H. Leonard Chapman for medicated hair tonic. A very nice turn-of-the-century piece priced at $500. *A steal*, she thought. She crossed out the *$500* and changed it to *$850*. She smiled to herself. She peeked over the top and saw the back of CC's head as she worked on the hot chocolate in the kitchen. On the 18th century drum table was a solid silver Russian samovar, used to serve tea perhaps at the imperial court. The silver gleamed. Anne ran her fingers along it, admiring its shiny surface and ornate floral carvings. It was a shame to part with it. She marked it up to *$500*, knowing it was unrealistic. She started feeling better about the sale.

She held up the Baccarat green art glass vase from 1900 that she'd found at the Paris flea market. She didn't even bother changing the price. She grabbed it and ran to her Mercury Mystique. When she came back, CC was carrying the urn full of steaming hot chocolate. "Where'd you go?" she asked, placing the chocolate on the counter.

"I was checking to see if any customers are here yet."

"I received 800 *will attends* on the Facebook event page."

"That's great," Anne said in a solemn voice.

CC went to check outside, the door was locked. "Anne, do you have the key?"

"Somewhere. I might have dropped it outside."

CC grabbed a letter opener from one of the displays, stuck it in the skeleton keyhole, popped open the lock, turned to Anne and said, "Really?" in a disapproving voice. It was a beautiful December morning, the sun was out, and it was unseasonably warm for a Chicago near winter. The parking spaces on the street filled up as a line formed outside the door. "There's no reason we can't let people in," CC said.

Anne checked her watch. "Five more minutes." Anne hurried back into the shop and closed the door behind her. She started hyperventilating. CC put her hands on Anne's shoulders. "Take a deep breath. We're going to have fun, and we're going to make a lot of people happy."

Anne looked over CC's shoulder at one of her favorite finds, a Pierre Jules Mene bronze sculpture of a fox. The room began to spin. "Fox," she mumbled, pointing.

"Anne, come sit down." CC led her to the pink velvet fainting couch.

Anne plopped down. "I guess we'll find a good home for everything. Aunt Sybil said these orphaned artifacts need to be loved and appreciated."

"That's right and all the people coming today are fans. Fans who've followed our adventures and supported us. Think of all the good you'll do today."

Anne glanced around CC's side at the Italian ice cream maker she'd found in the little French village. She closed her eyes. When she opened them, CC was inches away looking into them. "It's 9 a.m. Are you ready?"

Anne nodded her head. CC flipped open the lock and held the door wide open. Fans streamed in, each stopping to greet the Spoon Sisters, taking selfies, getting autographs. Anne was finally smiling, beaming in the attention. "Wait, put that down!" she exclaimed as someone balanced a rare Austrian Viennese enamel miniature tea service. Its surface was hand painted with 17th century courtiers. She rushed over to the woman to retrieve it. "Oh, that's a very rare find. It's in perfect condition and in its original box. It's lovely."

"How much is that? I cannot read without my glasses," the elderly woman said.

"I have it priced at $10,000," Anne said.

"Oh, my lord. I was looking for my granddaughter for when she plays tea party. I had no idea."

"Yes, it's very valuable. Everything in here is very valuable." Anne cradled the tea set in her arms before her attention was diverted. From behind her, a young couple was examining a 19th century German Meissen porcelain snowball cup with gold decoration. Anne recalled when she'd rescued it from an estate sale at a French castle on the outskirts of Paris.

The young woman examined it over carefully and said, "19th century. Very nice. Not even a nick on it. I see you have it marked a bit high here. Can you give me a better price?"

Anne stared at the price tag and then looked at the woman's Bulgari purse. This year's model. "Absolutely not. In fact, it's not even for sale. It's on hold for a customer." Anne reached over and took the cup from the young woman's hand. She cradled it and the tea set.

For the next half hour, CC greeted all their fans while Anne meandered around the store, picking up antiques and talking customers out of buying them. "What are you doing?" CC asked. "I've already sold five pieces."

"Which ones?" Anne asked, her eyes scanning the crowded room.

"That young man is coming back to pick up the fainting couch. That couple bought the armoire. They're going to turn it into an entertainment cabinet."

"Transform it? No, that won't do. You have to give them their money back." Anne sat on an armchair, breathing heavily. A little girl, no more than nine years old, came up to her holding a basket.

"Excuse me, ma'am," she said in a hesitant voice.

Anne looked at her. Her sparkling blue eyes and curly blond hair reminded her of herself at that age.

"You're Miss Hillstrom, aren't you? From the blog?"

"Yes." Anne nodded. "What's your name?"

"Dakota."

"Do you like antiques?"

"Yes, very much so. My mother and I read your blog every day. We go to garage sales and estates sales. I have a collection of original Nancy Drew books and Staffordshire dogs. I have nine of the original Wizard of Oz books."

"Those are my favorite, too," Anne said. "Do you know what that basket is you're holding?"

"No, it's really pretty. I thought I could put my dolls in it."

"That is a handmade French champagne grape pickers' basket from the early 1900s. It's called a Benaton from the champagne region of France. It's a thousand dollars."

"That's too much money." The girl's face fell.

"How much money do you have to spend?"

The little girl took out her change purse and counted out eight dollars. "I've been saving up my allowance."

"That's pretty good. I think we can find something you will like for eight dollars." Anne thought for a moment and remembered the French Mignonette doll she'd found in Lyons. "I think I have something in mind," Anne said. She stood up and walked to the corner where she'd placed the doll inside a curio cabinet. The little seven-inch doll signed by Jullien Jeune with its beautiful face, mohair wig, blue glass eyes and antique original dress and hat was worth at least $300. Anne had paid far less after finding the doll in a corner booth. She crossed out the $300 and wrote $8. She handed the doll to the girl. "What do you think of this doll?"

Dakota's eyes lit up. She hugged her. "She's beautiful." The little girl flipped the price tag over. "Eight dollars. I have eight dollars."

Anne smiled and walked her over to the cash register. She made her first sale of the day. After that, parting with her treasures was a little easier. She watched as each fan marveled over Anne's finds, appreciating their history and their beauty. It gave her a sensation she'd never felt before. Something that her Great Aunt Sybil had tried to instill in her. That the greatest value in collecting is sharing your collection with others. Just as her day couldn't get better, the door swung open.

Betsy Buttersworth and her silver sable coat flounced in. "Buttersworth," Anne muttered. The room grew still.

"Hillstrom," was her reply. The fans watched as though it was an old Western movie.

Betsy was not surrounded by her usual entourage, the ladies, as she referred to them. Instead she seemed to be alone. "Hillstrom, you have some very nice pieces. I remember when you bought that one." She pointed at a dry sink with a marble top. She reached over and ripped the tag off. "I see you've marked the prices up."

Anne watched in horror as Betsy made her way through the small shop, ripping tags right and left, leaving devastation behind her. This was not the sharing that Anne had in mind. Even Great Aunt Sybil would have drawn the line at Betsy Buttersworth. Anne couldn't watch. She ran out the front door to the porch and sat down in the wicker rocker, rocking almost as fast as her heart was beating. She could see Betsy's Bentley parked right in front of the building with someone sitting in the passenger side. Anne bent down to get a better look. She wondered why Betsy's friend was waiting in the car. She turned her head almost upside down for a better vantage point. All she could see was a long, bony hand hiding the face of the mysterious passenger. Wait, she recognized that hand. She ran down the porch, tapped on the window. The very tall British detective Nigel Towers lowered the window.

"Nigel, what are you doing in Betsy's car?" Anne asked.

"She asked me to come with her to the sale."

"Why would Betsy ask you to come with her?"

From behind her, Buttersworth said, "We're seeing each other."

Anne coughed and turned back to Nigel. His face was bright red. "Buttersworth?"

He nodded.

"Nigel and I have kept in contact since the Whitmore estate sale. He's been very supportive," Betsy said.

Anne turned back to Nigel. "Buttersworth?"

Betsy walked around to the driver's side of the car. Before getting in, she held up the price stickers. "Send me the bill and I'll have everything picked up." She tossed the tags into the air.

Anne caught the price tags.

Betsy got in the car and sped off. Anne stared, watching the tail lights as they disappeared around the corner of Pennsylvania Avenue. "Nigel and Buttersworth," she muttered, shaking her head.

"You have to do something about this traffic." The sweet shop lady stood in front of her, tapping her foot on the ground. The ashes from her cigarette danced as she waved it around. "There's no parking for blocks. My customers are complaining that they can't get to my store."

Anne glanced at her watch. "We'll be closing in ten minutes."

"You better." The sweet shop lady dropped the cigarette onto the sidewalk, crushing it with her heavy foot before waddling back to her store.

Anne climbed the steps back to the shop. The wind was taken out of her sails. She went back into the store. CC was ringing up purchases behind the counter. It had been a steady stream throughout the day. As Anne flipped the closed sign, a distinguished looking man rapped on the door, frightening her. "Sorry, we're closed," Anne said.

"I'm looking for an item," he said through the closed door.

"You'll have to come back next week," Anne replied. "We have to close today. Our city permit is very strict. We're having the second part of the sale next Saturday."

"I'm Professor Gildwin. I wrote you about the writing desk. I told you about the art school."

"I'm very sorry but I can't let you in." Anne pulled the shade over the door window and double locked it.

CC came out from the kitchen. "Who was that?"

"Just a last-minute customer. I told him to come back next week," Anne said.

They walked over to the register. CC handed Anne the stack of receipts and started counting the cash. "Add the receipts so we can tally the cash against it."

Anne reached into her bag for her calculator. She couldn't find it and dumped her bag onto the counter. Inside was her Waterman pen collection, antique porcelain thimbles, and Victorian hatpins. CC stood, staring. "Anne, I had those all listed on the presale. This one even has a tag." CC held up the Beaux Arts glass frame. "You put this in there today."

Anne didn't say a word.

"And what's this?" CC held up a silver jewel-encrusted serving knife.

Anne stared transfixed by the sparkle of the large green stone in the handle. "I don't remember where I got that from."

CC ran her finger along the square, blunt edge. "It looks very old. Either way we have to put all of these up for sale next week." CC took a picture of the serving knife and the frame to post on the blog.

Anne collected the smaller valuables and gave one last look at all the furniture still left. A large dent had been made in the room and there were plenty of bare spaces. "There's room for more next week. I'll get the pickup truck and come by for you before we come to the store," CC said.

They locked up the store. From the window next door, Anne could feel the glare of the sweet shop lady watching them. She didn't need to turn around.

Chapter Nine

CC drove the 1968 VW bus around the arrival circle at O'Hare Airport. She passed the long-term parking, then the day parking, then the hourly parking. When she saw the sign reading $9 an hour, she drove right past it. "What are you doing?" Anne asked.

"It's too much an hour," CC said. "I'm going to the long-term parking."

CC drove the three miles back to the long-term parking lot. "Isn't our time worth something?" Anne asked as they waited in the cold for the bus.

"The walk will do you good," CC said.

The bus dropped them off in front of terminal five, international arrivals, where they waited by baggage claim for Lufthansa. CC checked the arrival monitor over the bench where they sat. Anne checked her eBay watch list on her phone. "Her flight landed. She should be here soon," CC said.

The baggage carousel alarm went off, suitcases burst out through the tunnel. As the happy passengers grabbed their belongings, they took off. CC scanned the crowd for her cousin. "When was the last time you saw Ingrid?" Anne asked.

"Last time I was in Germany. Maybe ten years ago."

"Have you seen a recent picture of her?"

CC thought for a moment. "No, I never thought to ask."

As they spoke, a tall blonde Victoria's Secret model walked over and stood in front of them. "Hello, cousin," she said.

CC and Anne followed the line from the Doc Martin boots to the piercing sky blue eyes. "Ingrid?" CC said with a question mark.

"Ja." Ingrid nodded.

CC jumped up and gave the beautiful 18-year-old a hug. "My goodness, you've grown up," she said, looking her over.

Ingrid smiled. Anne shook her hand. "You probably don't remember me. We met when you came here that one summer with your family for the fourth of July. You were only six or seven."

"Ja, cousin CC's friend, Anne Hillstrom. I read your blog about both of you. My friends think I'm famous because I'm related to CC."

"Your English is very good," Anne said.

"It's really almost the first language in Germany. We're taught both in school."

Anne admired Ingrid's oversized calfskin bag. It resembled one she'd seen in the latest issue of *Vogue*. "I love your purse."

"It's a Rebecca Minkoff."

"That's right." Anne nodded. She remembered now. "It's very nice." She touched the soft calfskin.

Ingrid returned the favor. "Prada. This is the famous large, orange Prada bag from all the stories on the blog. May I touch it? You know my friends have matching large orange Prada bags in Munich."

Anne smiled. She put her arm around Ingrid. "We're going to have so much fun, you and I." As they walked to the parking lot, CC was left dealing with Ingrid's luggage. Anne continued, "Do you do much bargain hunting? Estate sales? Flea markets? In Germany?"

"How exciting. Yes. My friends and I go every weekend. All our clothes are vintage especially anything we can get American." She opened up her leather jacket, revealing a vintage Billy Idol concert t-shirt. She gave Anne a thumb and pinky up, a rebel yell sign.

"That's awesome," Anne said. "We'll have so much fun together."

CC struggled behind with a bag under each arm and a rolling suitcase. Ingrid stopped and took a big sniff of the air. "Oh, popcorn, can we stop?"

"We're going to be besties," Anne said. CC finally caught up.

The shuttle bus dropped them off at the long-term parking lot. Ingrid spotted the 68 VW and ran ahead. "I can't believe I'm seeing this in person. When I read that it was destroyed, my friends and I were so broken hearted. What fun adventures you two have had."

"It took a lot to get it back running," CC said.

Ingrid walked around, touching the German steel. "She looks beautiful." She pulled out her iPhone, stood by the side of the bus and took a selfie. Then she waved to Anne and posed with her in front of the bus. "Cousin CC, you think maybe I can drive her?"

CC thought for a moment. "We'll have to talk about that. I think O'Hare Airport is not a good place to start driving in Chicago."

"It can't be any worse than the Autobahn."

"That's kind of my point. You can't drive a hundred miles an hour, at least not legally, down the Kennedy. Let's get you back to my house and situated."

Ingrid pouted. Though Anne had not thought it possible, she was even more beautiful with her sad face. As Ingrid climbed in, CC walked over to Anne. "Anne, my gosh, what are we going to do with her? She's gorgeous. I'm responsible for keeping her out of trouble."

"She's like a young Heidi Klum," Anne agreed. "She'll be fine. We'll take her under our wing. I'll teach her."

"That's what I'm afraid of," CC whispered.

As they drove down the Tri-State back to Glen Ellyn, Anne pointed out the Chicago shopping mall with the outlet stores. "There's a Saks, a Neiman Marcus, Bloomingdale's and even Prada."

"Can we stop, cousin CC, please, can we stop?"

From the back seat, Anne repeated, "Can we stop, please?"

"No, I want to miss rush hour traffic," CC said.

Both Ingrid and Anne pouted.

CC pulled the bus up into the driveway of the split-level. Bandit watched patiently from the living room picture window. As CC went to the back of the bus to retrieve Ingrid's luggage, Anne walked her up to the front door. CC shook her head and dragged the bags out of the car and up to the doorway. She opened the door and let them in.

Bandit greeted them, wagging his tailless butt. Ingrid bent down, said, "Such a beautiful boy." She ran her fingers through his white soft furry chest. Bandit rubbed his head against her leg. Ingrid stood up and took a look around the living room. "This is very nice. Is this where I'll be staying?"

"Your bedroom is upstairs. Let me show you," CC said.

Anne and Ingrid flew up the steps as CC carried the suitcases behind them. CC had decorated the room with an old-fashioned white iron trundle bed. The quilt was the wedding ring pattern made by her grandmother. Patchwork pillows. A Lane cedar blanket chest was at the foot of the bed with another throw on top of it. She had added a small school desk, wooden chair and desk lamp. Anne had contributed a Mikasa vase with fresh flowers. "This is lovely, cousin CC, thanks for letting me stay here." Ingrid sat on the edge of the bed.

CC smiled. "I'm glad you're here. I think it's a good opportunity for you. I'm happy to help you."

Anne sat down on the small wooden chair. "So, you'll be attending Columbia College? That's a very good school."

"Yes, I want to be a writer."

"Like your cousin CC."

CC beamed.

Ingrid said, "No, I want to write fiction. Novels, love stories, cozy mysteries. I love Nancy Drew."

"Oh, I have such a large collection at my house. I'm going to bring them over for you. I'll bring you a bookcase, too," Anne said. "Oh, CC, I have that Globe Wernicke barrister bookcase I bought in Hickory. You think we could fit it in here?"

CC gazed around the small room. "We'll have to see, Anne."

"Oh, and she could help out with our pop-up sale. This is exciting." Anne jumped up and swirled around. She already started thinking about all the sales she could take Ingrid to. There was a viewing for Jennifer's Auctions on Saturday. Of course, she would be busy with her own sale but she could go to the viewing on Friday. "I'm going to start dinner," CC said.

Anne waved her off and sat on the bed next to Ingrid, showing her pictures of the upcoming auction on her iPhone.

CC could hear Anne and Ingrid chattering as she put oil on the fryer. She was making an American classic— fried chicken, mashed potatoes and apple pie. The chicken, of course, included her secret ingredient, just a hint of ghost pepper powder because it makes everything better. She washed and dried the chicken, dredged it in flour, put it in the buttermilk and dredged it in flour again. She tested the oil. It was sizzling so she dropped the chicken in it.

As the chicken cooked, she prepared the potatoes, mashing them with half and half, lots of Kerrygold grass-fed butter and her secret ingredient, softened cream cheese. She added a dash of her ghost pepper powder. When they were creamed, she tasted them and then added another dash of pepper. She had prepared the apple pie earlier.

While the chicken finished, she set the table, lit candles and then called up the stairs. "Dinner's ready."

Anne and Ingrid came flying down the stairs, giggling like a couple of sorority sisters. They sat at the table. CC opened a bottle of white wine. She poured a glass for herself and Anne. Ingrid looked surprised when CC didn't fill her glass. "You're only eighteen. In the United States, twenty-one is the drinking age."

"In Germany, we start having wine and beer for dinner at ten."

"While you're in the United States, let's follow the law," CC said.

Ingrid smiled and sipped her water. Anne giggled.

"CC, I was thinking back about the cake knife; I really don't remember buying it. Do you remember where we got it from?" Anne paused, thinking. "There was that one estate sale at the chateau where I got the Limoges platter. There were several crates. I bought them without knowing what was inside. They gave me a great price. I wonder." She paused again. "I opened all the crates and there's no matching pieces to the cake knife. I was hoping we'd find the matching pieces. At least maybe a cake platter."

"You could get more money for it if it was part of a matching set," CC said.

"I'm not sure I want to sell it. It's quite lovely." She pulled it out of her bag and cradled it.

"That is lovely. May I see it?" Ingrid asked. She examined the mother-of-pearl handle with its green stone inlay. "It's very old, isn't it?"

"Yes, it looks to be 18th century. You can tell by the stamp. I looked up that silversmith. It's definitely French mid- to late 18th century."

"What about the stone? What is it?"

"It's probably paste. If it was a real stone, I would have remembered paying a lot for it. Plus the bad news is if you turn it over the blade is pretty scratched up. I don't think we'll get much money for it. I might just keep it."

Ingrid handed the cake knife back to Anne who restored it back into her bag.

After clearing away the plates, CC returned to the dining room carrying a Dutch crumble apple pie. Ingrid bent over and breathed it in. "Mmm, this smells great."

CC went back and returned from the kitchen with an old-fashioned wooden hand-cranked ice cream machine. "I made the ice cream myself. French vanilla bean." She sliced up the pie, putting a generous scoop of ice cream on top which started to melt onto the cinnamon streusel topping. Anne gulped hers down. So much for her low-carb diet.

Ingrid leaned back in her chair, stretched her arms and gave a big yawn. It was only 8 p.m. but it had been a long flight.

"Ingrid, do you want to go lay down? You look tired."

She yawned again. "That's a good idea. Thank you, cousin CC." She kissed CC, then Anne and went upstairs.

CC stared at Anne in silence. Anne stared back with a confused look. "What? What are you looking at?"

"I haven't said a word. I was hoping you'd bring it up."

"What? Bring what up?" Anne stuck her finger in the empty bottom of the pie pan and licked it.

CC sat silent and then broke her silence. "Nigel and Betsy?"

"Oh, yes, at the sale. Nigel and Betsy. Apparently they're dating."

"When did this happen?"

"Apparently after I broke up with Nigel. Buttersworth scooped him up."

"I'm sorry. Are you okay with that?"

"Of course, I'm okay. Nigel and I are just friends now."

"Yeah, but Betsy?"

Anne tried to hide the fire rising inside her. She wanted to scream *Buttersworth* but was afraid she would wake Ingrid. "CC, thanks for dinner. I better get home to Sassy." Anne stood up, grabbed her bag and headed out to her car. Anne was so upset thinking about the very tall and very British ex-boyfriend dating her estate sale nemesis Buttersworth, she didn't notice the headlights that followed her home.

Chapter Ten

Anne couldn't take it any longer. She had to go to the store and rescue the rescued items. She couldn't part with the alabaster lamp or the gold ormolu mantle clock. As she drove to the store, she muttered, "Buttersworth." She thought about the vintage Welsh oak chest. "Buttersworth," she muttered again. The 1800s era coal miner's three compartment lunch bucket. "Buttersworth." She pressed her foot on the gas, beginning to realize it wasn't giving up the antiques that was gnawing at her, it was giving up Nigel. Not just giving him up, but giving him to Buttersworth. "Buttersworth!" she screamed. The family in the minivan next to her at the red light turned and looked in horror. The young girl in the booster seat began to cry. Anne pressed on.

She parked her Mercury Mystique in the lot behind the store, squeezing it next to the dumpster. She had three hours before CC and Ingrid would show up for today's sale. Enough time to make a few trips back to her house. Or, maybe she should rent a storage locker closer to the store. A light snow began to fall as she went up to the back door of the store. She sniffed the air. She could smell caramel. Must be coming from next door. *Mmm, caramel,* she thought. She took a deeper whiff. *Mint and caramel? Yuck. I won't be buying any caramels from her. Who puts mint in caramel?* She glanced over next door at the sweet shop. A white cloud of smoke billowed up through the back door. The caramel was burning. She squeezed between the dumpster and the little fence and pounded on the back door of the sweet shop. The smell and the smoke intensified. Anne coughed. She took her elbow and knocked the glass out of the back door. She reached inside and unlocked it. Flames rose up from the kitchen. Anne ducked down and held her Burberry scarf over her nose. "Sweet shop lady, are you there? Are you there?" Anne yelled. She couldn't see through the smoke. She could hear sirens in the distance. As the smoke parted, all she could make out in the kitchen was a large stainless steel mixing vat. Rising out of it were a pair of size nine orthopedic extra wide Dr. Scholl's. The sweet shop lady had been Augustus Gloopified just like in *Charlie and the Chocolate Factory*. Unlike Augustus, the sweet shop lady had not survived: death by caramel.

Anne backed out of the burning building as the fire engines pulled up in front. "Ma'am, stand back. Are you all right?" A paramedic ran up to her, pulling her away from the building.

"Caramel. Sweet shop lady!" Anne's breath came out in short bursts as she pointed toward the store. The paramedic brought her over to the ambulance. He sat her down and checked her vitals.

"Ma'am, do you want us to call anyone?"

"Nigel." She handed him her iPhone.

The paramedic searched the contact list, reaching Nigel. A union jack appeared. Nigel answered. The EMT explained what happened. As the Glen Ellyn Fire Department extinguished the fire, Anne watched as they wheeled out the covered body of the sweet shop lady. Burnt caramel dripped down the sides of the gurney. She turned her head away, trying not to look. An unmarked police car pulled up.

Detective Nigel Towers leaped out, rushing over to Anne. He bent down, putting his hands on her shoulders. "Annie, are you okay?" he asked.

Anne looked up with a tear in her eye. "It was horrible, Nigel, horrible. There was smoke, caramel and fire." She stood up and wrapped her arms around him, hugging him, her head barely higher than his chest. Nigel lightly tapped her back and then held her firmly. Anne pulled away slowly. "I'm so sorry to have called you but I didn't know what to do."

"I'm glad you did. Have you spoken to the police?"

"No, they're still rummaging through the ruins. Ohmigosh, our sale today. We're having our second pop-up sale." Anne glanced at the half-burnt sweet shop, a crowd was gathering on the sidewalk in front. Down the street, she could see the fluorescent green and white smiling face of CC's 1968 VW bus. She looked back at Nigel. And, then she remembered why she'd come early to the store.

"I don't think you'll be opening your store today. They'll be investigating and roping off this whole area."

Anne let out a sigh of relief.

"Oh, don't be sad, I'm sure you'll be able to have your sale in a couple of days."

Anne sighed again, but this time in frustration. "Nigel, I'm really shook up. Do you think maybe we could have dinner tonight and talk about all this? I could tell you about my trip to France and . . . ?"

"I do have plans for tonight." Nigel hesitated, glanced again at Anne's tear-stained face. He had never stopped caring for her. Truth be told, he had never stopped loving her. "I guess I can change my plans."

"That's very sweet of you," Anne said. "I'm very shook up."

"Anne, are you okay," CC exclaimed, running up to Anne. "I heard about the fire this morning while I was listening to the police and fire dispatch. What happened?"

"I got here early to get ready for the sale. The sweet shop was on fire. I called out to the sweet shop lady. When she didn't answer, I went inside to see if she was in there. And she was." Anne shuddered, recalling the image.

"I know. It's horrible," CC said, putting her arms around her friend.

"It is horrible." Anne hesitated. "I guess we'll have to cancel the sale."

"Yes, we'll have to reschedule."

"Or cancel?"

"We'll talk about when to reopen. The important thing is you're okay. We'll get you home so you can rest."

"I don't feel like going home. I'm pretty shook up. I need to get my mind off this."

"Sure, whatever you want to do."

Anne thought for a moment. "Actually, there are a couple of sales I wanted to check out. I thought because we did so well at the last pop-up, we could add a couple items and do a quick flip."

CC didn't have the heart to tell Anne all the things that were wrong with that statement. She agreed. Ingrid sat quietly. An attractive young Glen Ellyn fireman walked over to them. His short black hair bordering on blue accented his deep blue eyes. He was tall, muscular. Soot dotted his chiseled face. "Miss Hillstrom, we have all the information we need right now. The police will contact you if they need anything else." He glanced over at Ingrid. "Ma'am, did you witness the fire?"

"Oh, no, I just got here." She shook her head.

The handsome young fireman smiled. "Is that an accent I hear?"

"Yes, I'm from Germany. I came to America to study."

"That's really interesting."

Ingrid's sparking blue eyes locked the fireman's gaze. He couldn't stop smiling. He took off his glove. "My name is Adam." He shook her hand, not letting go.

"Ingrid," she said with a shy smile.

"Listen, Ingrid, I have to get back to work. I'd love to get your number and show you around Chicago."

She smiled again. CC stood up and pulled their hands apart. "Ingrid, we have to get going." Ingrid smiled; the young fireman smiled back. Anne said goodbye to Nigel, arranging to meet him later. The three antique hunters piled into the VW.

Anne concealed her enthusiasm from CC. She read off the directions to the first sale to CC as she drove. "Now, Ingrid, this estate sale is not in someone's home. The company running it had so many items that they rented a warehouse and moved everything there."

"That's exciting," Ingrid said.

"I'm not sure what we'll find there. I want you to stick close to me but if you see something, grab it because otherwise someone else will." Anne smoothed her flowered Capri pants, remembering the day she found them. It was at such a sale as the one she was going to, very high-end, very good pieces.

"What am I looking for?" Ingrid asked.

Anne pulled out a large binder from her bag. "You can help us find items listed in this book. These are requests from our fans. I have them cataloged according to type so you'll find sections for crystal, collectibles, china, household goods, furniture and even sports. Then I have them further divided by era. Some of the fans will be coming to the pop-up store, that is, if we reopen."

"That's really exciting. This is so fun."

CC glanced in the rearview mirror at her cousin, sitting in the back seat, smiling. She had a look in her eye. A look she'd seen before. She turned and looked at Anne who had the same look. That's where she'd seen it before. The look was a mixture of excitement and anticipation, bordering on obsession.

Anne pointed down a country road in an area lined with prefab warehouses. She could see the line of cars before they even turned the corner. Many were parked haphazardly along the drainage ditch as the parking lot in front of the warehouse was full. Some people were already leaving, carrying items. Anne stared longingly at a large floor lamp with an elephant base being carried out by an enthusiastic young couple. They were too late. CC parked the VW. Anne jumped out, followed by Ingrid.

Entering the warehouse, there was a line of folding banquet tables with small household items like crystal, pottery, china and collectibles. "This is the estate of Margaret Reed. She had a large house in Geneva that had been in her family for more than a hundred years. The house is being torn down so the company is having the sale here," Anne explained to Ingrid as she examined a Belleek vase. She put it back down.

"What we're looking for today are items that will sell quickly at the pop-up sale and for items on our list. The more smalls the better. They take up less real estate and people are more likely to buy them if they can take them home the same day."

CC went off toward the garden area where there was a large wrought iron gazebo, some jardinière pots. She studied a marble pot on a brass stand. Egyptian revival. It must date back to the 1920s, she thought. She tried to lift it but it was very heavy. She studied it, walking around it. It would look perfect next to her front door with a Boston fern.

Anne, followed by Ingrid, moved along the expansive warehouse floor, which was overflowing with furniture. They first came to a Chippendale style chair. "This is really beautiful," Ingrid said.

Anne took a look, examining it from all angles. "It's the right style and the right size. Let's look a little closer, starting with the back splat. That's where you sit with your back up against the chair. See how the back looks like a vase?"

Ingrid ran her hand along the wood back splat. "Is that what tells us that it's a real Chippendale?"

"No, but it helps us date the chair. Don't look at the positive space, which is the piece of wood that looks like a vase on the chair back. Instead study the negative space, the cutout. Do you see that the negative space looks like two birds in profile gazing at each other?"

Ingrid took a step back, staring at the cutout. "Yes, I see that now. I never would have noticed that. It does look like two birds facing each other."

"The beak tells you not only where it was manufactured but also helps you date it. The most desirable Chippendale style chair dates back to early Colonial America. The secret is in the length of the beak." Anne ran her finger along the beak of the curved open wood. "A short beak means it was made in Massachusetts or Rhode Island. A longer beak means it was made in Philadelphia."

"This looks like a flamingo. Where would that be from?" Ingrid asked.

"Because it looks like a flamingo, it is overdone. It's a reproduction. It's not an authentic Chippendale or early American Chippendale style," Anne said. "We're not interested. Let's move on."

Ingrid took out a small reporter's notebook and jotted notes down. Anne could hear her mumbling in German as she wrote.

Later, they went back to the table overflowing with various pieces of china. Anne picked up a piece of porcelain. "Don't worry about the marks. Look at the foundation of the clay, the color. The best clay is bright white like this one. It even has 22 karat gold banding, This plate is worth about $30, it's marked $8. We'll take it."

"It's the opposite with silver." Anne picked up a silver fork. "If it says sterling or .925, then we know it's silver. If your piece has a lion symbol looking left, it also means it's sterling. That's the English hallmark for sterling. If it doesn't have a mark, it's usually plate."

Ingrid scribbled quickly in her notepad. Next Anne picked up a piece of pottery, a very nice Chinese ceramic vase, white with purple lotus blossoms. She handed it to Ingrid. "What do you feel?"

Ingrid felt the weight of the vase. "I don't know. What should I be feeling?"

"Sometimes there's just something cheap to the look and feel of imitation vases. Handmade pottery has an unglazed bottom so you see the natural clay. Before firing of the pottery, it's dipped in a fast-drying glaze. The potters wipe the bottom clean so they won't have to clean their instruments. The potter also uses pincers to hold the handmade pottery so you should look at the sides to see if you can see any pincer marks. This will give you a good indication that it wasn't mass produced in a town in China but painstakingly, lovingly crafted by an artist by hand." Anne paused. "I took a pottery class at the College of DuPage, an eight-week course so I could understand the process of creating pottery. It helped me understand how a forger would try to create an imitation, what to look for."

Ingrid smiled and scribbled in her notebook.

"Yes, we can take a class together," Anne said.

Next to the table of household goods was a large plastic bin overflowing with purses. Anne rifled through them. Ingrid pulled out a small orange bag. "Look, it's like yours." She held it up.

Anne took it from her and examined the purse. The color of the triangular logo on the front was a near match to the purse color and was firmly attached with even stitching. "See, Ingrid, you can tell this is a vintage Prada because the rivets look like donut holes. In the new bags, they are filled in." Anne glanced inside the purse. She showed the label to Ingrid. "This is good. It's their three-line label saying Prada, Milano, Made in Italy. The new bags only have two lines. And, its color matches the interior color." Anne then checked the back of the zipper. "Lampo," it read on the backside. "This appears to be an original Prada zipper. They only use a few zippers, and Lampo is one. And, all the hardware says Prada. This definitely appears to be authentic. This is a very good find, Ingrid."

Ingrid put the purse over her shoulder, twisting this way and that, admiring herself. "See, like you, Anne."

"Yes, we're purse sisters," Anne said, giggling.

CC put a sold tag on the marble plant pot resting on its brass stand after she negotiated a price with the manager. Glancing up, she saw the purse sisters walking down the aisle, laughing. Anne was having a good time. She hadn't noticed the perfectly coiffed $300 hairdo haggling at the jewelry display until she bumped into it. "Buttersworth!" she exclaimed.

Betsy Buttersworth spun around, standing nose to nose with "Hillstrom." Betsy noticed Ingrid. "What's this? Little Hillstrom?"

"Hello, nice to meet you, I'm Ingrid Muller. Wait, you're Betsy Buttersworth? I read in Cousin CC's blog about you and Anne and the Packwell sale and the pants."

Betsy turned a paler shade of red.

"And, I read about you and your fiancé."

Betsy turned a deeper shade of red.

Anne nudged Ingrid.

"I was disappointed you had to cancel the second pop-up sale. I enjoyed rummaging through all your hand-me-downs," Betsy said.

Anne thought to herself, *hand-me-downs like Nigel.* Instead she said, "We'll be having another one next Saturday. In fact, we're looking for more merchandise for the store."

"Oh, is this a permanent thing now? I thought you were having a closeout sale. I heard you were having financial problems."

Anne's face turned red. She counted to ten in her head. Ingrid watched as her lips moved. Ingrid counted along, with her lips moving also. "Anne was teaching me how to identify imitation antiques. For instance, that vase you're holding is not a very good piece. The color is more off white than white." Ingrid pulled a pen flashlight out of her purse and shined the light through the vase. "You can see where it's been broken and patched. The rest of the vase is translucent. Here there's a dead spot where the light doesn't shine through." Ingrid turned to Anne and gave her a knowing wink. "I read that on the Spoon Sisters blog."

Betsy put the vase down and walked away. "Buttersworth, no relation to the syrup but still a sticky problem," Ingrid said.

Anne giggled.

CC came up to them. "What have you two been up to? I found a couple things. There's an old brass birdcage that I thought we could hang in the front window of the store. I also found something I wanted to get your opinion on. It's not politically correct but then again I don't know if it's our place to make that decision on something that was made a hundred years ago when it was politically correct." CC walked back to the part of the warehouse that held the large pieces. Ingrid and Anne followed her.

Standing right in front was a six-foot-tall cigar store Indian carved out of white oak. The paint on the full headdress and feathers was a bit faded but very intricate. Anne circled around thinking of John Blackbear. She touched the muscular bare arms, tribal drums pounded in her head as John Blackbear, her summer fling, pounded in her heart. "I don't know, CC, I appreciate the craftsmanship and I appreciate the time it came from but are we perpetuating a negative stereotype?" Anne took a picture and texted her friend, Chief John Blackbear who lived in Cherokee, North Carolina.

"What are you doing?" CC asked.

"I think John Blackbear might appreciate this in an odd kind of way," Anne said. "He collects Smoky Mountain antiques and if you notice by the signature, it's dated 1865, Cherokee, North Carolina." Her iPhone dinged. The text read, "I'm intrigued both by the statue and that you contacted me. Would like to see both." Anne smiled and blushed a bit. "Let's buy it."

As they were paying for their items at the estate sale, CC's phone rang. "Hello," she answered. She carried on a conversation quietly while Anne rifled through her bag for her change purse. After a few moments, she hung up.

"Who was that?" Anne asked.

"That was Professor Gildwin. He wanted to see if he could come pick up the drawing desk."

"No," Anne said.

"I promised it to him."

"I have plans for it."

"What kind of plans?"

"Plans that don't involve you."

"Why are you being so snippy?" CC asked.

"I'm not being snippy. I have agreed to sell off all or almost all of my antiques from Paris. I'm even going to clear out my garage and the storage lockers but at some point there's a couple things I want to keep for myself."

"I can understand that. You've been very brave," CC said.

"Yes, I have been very brave."

"I'm sure we can find him some other items from the art school. I'll tell him we'll hold them and won't sell them at the sale until he's looked at them. I'll call him back."

Anne and Ingrid struggled with the tobacco store Indian, carrying him out to the VW bus while CC called the professor back.

Chapter Eleven

Anne strolled into the brightly lit, brightly colored Carnivale restaurant. Lively Latino music greeted her, rising above the clatter of voices and clinking of glasses. The entry was crowded; she pushed her way through to the hostess stand. The hostess led her to a table in the dining room. Anne was transfixed by the décor; it was bright and lively. The ceiling was decorated with multi-colored glass tiles. She felt as if she was in Rio. She sat on a big overstuffed striped red and gold velvet chair across from Nigel. On the small stage, scantily clad women danced the samba, the Brazilian dance with African influences. Anne tapped her foot and shimmied her shoulders.

Nigel smiled. "Do you want to dance?"

"Oh, no, no."

Anne stared at Nigel. He was handsome, dressed for the occasion in his hot pink silk shirt which matched the walls. He reached across the table and held Anne's hand. "How are you?"

Anne continued to watch the dancers on the stage, tapping her foot. "What? What?" she asked as she turned back to Nigel.

"I said, how are you?"

Anne smiled. "I'm fine. I'm doing just fine."

"You seemed very upset this morning. I was worried about you."

"This morning?" Anne thought for a moment and then said, "I was. I mean I am." She let go of Nigel's hand and took a sip of her water.

The waitress came by, introduced herself. "Can I interest you in a cotton candy cocktail? It's our signature drink."

"What's in it?"

"Purity vodka, lime, grapefruit and cotton candy."

"Yum. I'll take one."

Nigel glanced over the drink menu she'd handed to him and ordered a mojito. As the waitress started to turn, Anne said, "Can we order some appetizers now while you're here?"

"Of course," the waitress said.

Anne quickly skimmed the list, passing over the Amazonian chopped salad, which was all greens, tomatoes and dates, the Caesar salad, pausing momentarily at the coconut shrimp, and finally landing at the Ropa Vieja. "This sounds delicious, Nigel, braised brisket, sweet plantains, malanga and queso fresco. Armallo aioli."

Nigel nodded in agreement. As the waitress started to walk away again, Anne said, "Wait. Can we get an order of Charcuterie and cheeses?"

The waitress nodded and left.

"I'm starving," Anne said. "I haven't eaten all day. I've been on a diet since I returned from Paris."

"How was Paris? You never told me."

"Oh, Nigel, it was so beautiful. I didn't want to come back. The shops, the food, the museums and our hotel were fantastic. Did I tell you that Bradley from the Hermitage in Nashville helped us? I've kept in touch. We write each other once a week, not emails mind you, but handwritten letters. He's very old school. That's a delightful way to read. Anyway when I told him I was going to Paris, he referred me to the concierge at the King George, a friend of his from his luxury hotel concierge network. Jean-Paul was wonderful and took great care of us. He got us tickets for the opera, reservations for the best restaurants, private showings at the museums."

"I'm really glad you had a good time," Nigel said. "But I'm more glad you came home." Nigel ran his bony fingers along her hand.

Anne sighed. "Yes, home. And that leads me to why I'm selling off my beautiful souvenirs. Somebody stole my identity. They hacked into my savings account and took all my money."

"That's bloody awful."

The waitress brought their drinks. Anne took a big gulp. "That's really good." She took another big sip. "You better bring another," she said to the waitress before turning back to Nigel. "Speaking of the sale, did you find anything out about the sweet shop lady and the fire?"

"One of the paramedics told me she drowned in the caramel vat. There's no official cause of death but I saw the body," Nigel said.

"What about the fire?"

"Stella, that was her name, fell into the vat, which jammed up the mixing blade, overloading the motor which caused a short in the wiring. The fire started inside the walls."

"That's horrible," Anne said.

The waitress set down the appetizers on the table and a second cotton candy drink. Anne finished off the plate of artisan cheeses and meats, pausing before starting on the second appetizer. Anne looked up; Nigel hadn't touched a thing. "Nigel, what's wrong? How come you're not eating?"

"I came here tonight because I thought you were upset. I thought you needed a friend. I wanted to be that friend. You don't look very distraught."

"I eat when I'm nervous."

Nigel thought she must be nervous a lot. He gazed at his watch, and then he looked over Anne's shoulder to see Betsy Buttersworth walking in the door. Anne followed his gaze, a piece of meat dangling from her mouth. "Buttersworth," she spat out the words and the meat.

Betsy knelt down and kissed Nigel on the cheek, sitting on the bench next to him. "Hillstrom," she said.

Anne stared in disbelief.

"Nigel told me how upset you were. When he told me he was meeting you for dinner, I wanted to come and lend my support," Buttersworth said, holding a martini glass. She then turned her gaze to Nigel. "Nigel, Anne and I bumped into each other earlier today at an estate sale."

Nigel didn't say a word.

The waitress came back to the table, asking Betsy if she wanted to order another drink.

"No," Betsy said.

The waitress stood, waiting for their order.

Anne stood. "You know I'm not feeling so well. I think I'm going to go."

Nigel stood up, bumping his knees on the table. "Wait, Anne."

Anne ran out of the building, bumping into the samba dancers and a cocktail waitress and leaving a devastation of glitter and drinks in her wake.

Chapter Twelve

Anne sat on the rocker in her screened-in back porch. She sipped her tea, hoping the hot liquid would stave off the chill from the early winter cold. Sassy, the mother-to-be, lay on her 17th century Brussels tapestry pillow, purring. Anne sighed, the pillow another treasure she might have to relinquish. With the proceeds from the first sale, she'd paid her mortgage but not the rest of her bills. Her credit cards were maxed out. The bank was certainly taking its time resolving her identity theft crisis. Obviously, it was not a crisis for them but a monumental one for her. She'd filled out countless documents, had them notarized and made constant phone calls to them. They assured her they were working on the situation as fast as they could but it was complicated because it involved foreign banks, retail locations and a well-used account. She was in dire straits.

All three containers had been cleared out and removed from her driveway. Between Craigslist, eBay and the pop-up sale, she'd exhausted her inventory. She looked across the driveway into her two-car detached garage. Inside was her last bastion. Her keep of keepsakes. Tomorrow was the next pop-up sale. They had received clearance from the police and fire departments so they could reopen. Everything in the store had interest from fans who'd seen the pictures CC had posted.

Anne opened her bag and took out her perfume bottles. She unwrapped each one, stopping to admire it.

She held the delicate Bohemian art deco perfume bottle with its root beer brown glass color. Next was the L'Air du Temps Lalique perfume bottle with its carved dove stopper, signed by the artist. At the bottom of the bag, she felt the cool silver of the antique cake knife. She retrieved it, marveling at its craftsmanship and the green stone. She wished she could remember where she'd found it. Provenance was everything. She pulled out her loupe, holding it up to her eye, gazing at the stone for the first time. Where she expected to see clear glass, instead she saw tiny fissures. She checked again to make sure her eyes weren't deceiving her. Those were definitely fissures, and they were needlelike, not flattened as though they'd been treated. It was a real emerald, and from what Anne knew from her brief online course at the Gemology Institute of America, it was a very fine quality emerald. It had to be at least five carats. Her hand started to shake a bit.

She pulled her iPhone out of her bag and Googled the price of a five-carat near flawless emerald. She looked over the knife with a new eye. This was a very special cake knife. The stone alone had to be worth a $100,000. Where did she find it? She couldn't have paid what it was worth. She couldn't afford this knife. Had she gotten such a deal in her shopping frenzy that she couldn't remember? Out of a thousand antiques she bought in Paris, she remembered 999. When? Where? She could not remember this piece.

She examined the handle. Stamped into it was a small crowned fleur de lis, with two small dots on either side. If she remembered her antiques correctly, this mark was an early 18th century mark used in Paris to identify it as pure silver. She wrapped it in her Hermes scarf and put it back in her bag. She held the bag to her chest. This could be the answer to all her financial problems. But then again how could she part with it? A piece this valuable must have a history. She decided to unravel its secret before even thinking about selling it. She felt better as she rocked, sipping her tea. She was on the trail of an antique mystery.

Sassy lifted her head, barely having the strength to purr. Her due date was near. It reminded Anne that there would soon be new mouths to feed.

Ingrid stepped up the driveway and knocked on the screen door. Anne sat up with a start. She had forgotten that Ingrid had offered to help clear out the garage.

Ingrid came into the porch, knelt down and pet Sassy. Sassy rolled over onto her back, not Sassy's usual posturing. "Anne, thank you so much for letting me help today. I can't wait to see what's inside your garage."

"Me too. Would you like some tea before we get started?" Anne asked, reaching for the teakettle which was on the wicker coffee table.

"What a beautiful kettle. It looks very old."

"Sit." Anne pointed to the white wicker rocking chair that was the mate to the one she was sitting in. As Ingrid rocked, Anne thought of her Great Aunt Sybil who had once occupied that chair. "Yes, this tea kettle was gifted to me by my Great Aunt Sybil."

"Yes, I remember reading that. That's the Sherlock Holmes kettle."

"Yes, Sir Arthur Conan Doyle. It's steeped many a great tea and many a great mystery. My aunt told me how she found this kettle at an estate sale in Crowborough, England, where Doyle lived with his second wife, Jean Leckie. Sybil traveled there after World War II to ease the pain of the loss of her fiancé. Sybil was a great lover of mysteries, especially Sherlock Holmes. She was drawn to the love story of Doyle and Jean Leckie. That story took her to Crowborough where Doyle lived out his days with Jean

Leckie. He'd been in love with her but he'd kept their relationship platonic because his first wife Mary Louise was sick. He married Jean Leckie after Mary Louise died from tuberculosis. My aunt loved the romance of the story."

"How did she find the kettle?" Ingrid asked, clutching her teacup.

"The estate sale was held by his great grandchildren. Most of the items for sale were tagged and priced. There was one room roped off with *Do Not Enter* so, of course, Great Aunt Sybil snuck in, just for a peek, mind you." Anne recalled her spoon. "Anyway, the room was full of broken chairs, dirty linens, items they couldn't sell, meant to be thrown out. That's when she saw a bit of the shiny copper peeking out from a bare wood shelf. It was dented, tarnished and absolutely wonderful. She rescued the orphaned artifact, left to be an erased memory." Anne lifted the teakettle. "You can see his initials. The story goes his second wife gave the kettle to him before they were married. It reminded Great Aunt Sybil of her departed fiancé, the love story, that is. Sometimes when I use it, I imagine Sir Arthur sitting next to me telling me his ideas for new Sherlock Holmes adventures."

"What a wonderful story. So sad about Great Aunt Sybil and her lost love." Ingrid smiled. "She sounds like an amazing woman. I would have liked to have gone shopping with her."

"I feel like she's still with me, especially when I'm antique hunting. She taught me everything I know about antiques." Anne recalled her great aunt who was not very well liked by many. Anne had a close relationship with her because of their shared fondness for old things. "Should we get started?"

"Yes, please." Ingrid stood up with youthful enthusiasm. She followed Anne to the garage. Anne hefted the large overhead door, revealing the teetering mounds of treasures. Standing next to her, Ingrid stared in awe.

Anne placed her hands on her hips and surveyed the contents. She had no clue where to start. "The dragon chair on top looks like early Chinese," Ingrid said. "Are you thinking about selling that at the store?"

Anne recalled the day she'd tied it to the top of her car and brought it home. It had been a tremendous effort. "It's in need of repair. We'll put that on the maybe list."

Ingrid climbed up the mountain of boxes and furniture and lifted it off its perch. "Let's put it to the side for now." She brought it outside, putting it on the driveway. Anne sat in it, staring into the garage. "How about this waterfall bedroom set? It's very nice. Is that about 1920s?" Ingrid opened the drawer. "These look like Bakelite handles."

"That's right, Ingrid, very good. That was my grandparents'. That stays."

Ingrid climbed nearly to the top of the garage. "Oh, this desk, this is really neat." She struggled, carrying it down. She looked it over, the four-foot French white oak top flipped over. "This is neat. You can adjust the angle of the top like a drafting table."

"It's a school desk but at the art school they referred to it as a drawing desk. That's why the top is so wide. It can handle different canvas sizes. It angles up almost like an easel when the students are sketching live models."

Ingrid walked around it, looking it over. "Is this for sale?"

Anne thought a moment. "Well, I was thinking about cleaning it up and giving it to CC for Christmas."

Ingrid smiled. "Yes, I've seen her art studio in her house. This would be a perfect fit but it's pretty scratched up. I can help you restore it. My father taught me."

Anne jumped up, horrified, interrupting, "Absolutely not. This table is mid-19th century. All those scratches were from art students that passed through a famous art school in Paris. Who knows who sat there?"

"There are some initials here, J.C.T."

"Yes, I saw those but I couldn't match those with anyone famous. Probably some kid who never made a name for himself. It's still a very cool historical item. All I'd do is use a little Murphy's soap to clean it up."

Ingrid left the desk on the driveway, climbed back on top of the piles. Tied to the rafters was an empire-style crystal, brass and enamel chandelier. Ingrid sat on the top of the mountaintop, looking up, touching the crystal. "Anne, how about this chandelier? I can reach it. Do you want me to bring it down?"

Anne thought for a moment. That chandelier was from the Whitmore estate sale. It had too much history. It was the beginning of the Spoon Sisters blog and their fame. It was the beginning of her new life and it was the first time she met Nigel. "No, no, no. Leave it there. Don't touch it."

Ingrid snapped her hand back, staring down at Anne. "Anne, have you noticed the drawing on the desk?"

"What are you talking about?" Anne got up from her throne, walked over by the desk. "I don't see what you're talking about. It's just a bunch of scratches."

"From up here, they all form a drawing." Ingrid took her iPhone and snapped a picture. She slalomed down and showed Anne.

"Wow." Anne flipped the desk to a ninety-degree angle and walked down the driveway, stopping about 10 feet away. She turned to see a perfect reproduction scratched into the white oak of Seurat's *A Sunday Afternoon on the Island of La Grande Jatte*, more commonly known as *Sunday in the Park*. She knew it well from her many visits to Chicago's world-famous Art Institute. The bustled ladies with their parasols, the picnicking couple on a blanket watching the tiny sailboats and even the monkey at the lady's feet were all painstakingly recreated in the etching. She walked back and examined the top up close. "The whole etching is tiny dots, copied exactly like Seurat in the pointillist style. This student was really bored and really talented. CC's going to love this. I wish I knew who this J.C.T. was. Obviously he was a good artist for a copycat."

The morning continued much the same. Ingrid climbing up the piles, dragging down antiques. Anne shaking her head, *No.* By late afternoon, Anne and Ingrid had managed to make *yes*, *maybe* and *definitely not* piles. The *yes* pile was the smallest of the three. "Well, this should put a dent in things. Some of the items in the *yes* pile have been spoken for by our fans. The desk I'm keeping. But the easel and the paintbrushes are from the same sale at the art school. I think the one fan who told us about the sale should be happy with those." Anne did a calculation in her head and thought the *yes* pile should take care of two months of mortgage, enough time for the bank to clear up her identity theft problem and restore her funds. "So, Ingrid, what do you have planned for tonight?"

"Actually I got a phone call from Adam, you know, the cute fireman we met at the sweet shop." Ingrid smiled. "He invited me to go bowling at Pinstripes. It's a bar and bowling alley."

"Oh, that sounds like fun."

"Yes, but I don't know what to wear."

Anne thought for a moment. "I think this calls for a break. There's a vintage dress shop at Harlem and Irving in Chicago. It's called Katrina's. We'll find you something there." Anne ran to her 1992 Mercury Mystique, clearing out the passenger side while Ingrid placed everything back inside the garage.

Ingrid jumped in the car. Anne headed east down Irving Park Road into the city. Anne glanced sideways at Ingrid, evaluating her color palette, age and body. "You're lucky, Ingrid, anything will look nice on you. On one hand, if you're bowling, pants might be more comfortable, but if you want to impress this guy maybe we can find you a skirt. One of the fondest memories my Great Aunt Sybil had that she told me about many times as a little girl was the night she went bowling with her fiancé before he shipped off to the war. I have a piece of the bowling alley where they stood on their last night together. There's something very Americana and romantic about a bowling date."

Anne parked the car on the street in front of Katrina's. They went into the small boutique. Ingrid sorted through the racks of silks and satins. "This is it." Anne pulled out a pair of dark blue high-waisted sailor pants. "Katherine Hepburn. Ingrid, these with a silk lace blouse, it says beautiful, yes, but strong and independent, too."

Ingrid grabbed the pants and a sheer white top with a white camisole. She went into the small changing room. When she came out, Anne had a red silk scarf draped around her neck with a pair of heart-shaped sunglasses. "Oh, Ingrid, you look adorable. You have to get them." Anne found a pair of vintage Bohemian crystal earrings with a matching blue necklace. She turned Ingrid so she was facing the mirror. "See, perfect."

"Oh, Anne, you're right." Ingrid hugged Anne.

After they paid for their purchases, they walked a few blocks to a little Greek diner. Before the waitress could ask, Anne said, "Saganaki and two Diet Cokes, please."

"You think cousin CC is going to be upset about my date?" Ingrid sipped at her Diet Coke.

Anne giggled. "With a Glen Ellyn fireman? How could she possibly be upset?"

"She feels responsible for me. I think she still sees me as a little girl."

"There's no way anyone can see you as a little girl, Ingrid."

The waitress lit the cheese, exclaimed, "Opa," and set it on the table. Anne scraped her knife into the steel-serving pan. Ingrid squeezed lemon juice and sopped up the cheesy juice with her Greek bread. "Adam. He's new on the force. He's only 24."

"He was very cute," Anne said, recalling seeing him the day of the fire. "Have you talked a lot?"

"Not during the day because I'm in school, but he called me late last night. He's going to come to your next sale. He's looking for antique fire equipment and gear to decorate the bar with."

"Bar?"

"Adam's opening a bar with some of his friends from the firehouse. A fireman themed bar. Someplace to go after their shifts or softball games. He's going to show me the building after we bowl."

"Mmm, let me think." Anne thought for a moment. "I've got a vintage oxygen mask. Oh, wait a minute, I have a vintage Harden's star glass grenade fire extinguisher. It's on a plaque. They could hang it on a wall." Anne sopped up the rest of the grease with her bread. "And, there's a warehouse in Chicago; it's by Maxwell Street. Are you familiar with Maxwell Street?"

Ingrid sipped her Diet Coke and shook her head.

"Maxwell Street is on the near south side of Chicago. It was an open flea market for blocks of anything you wanted to buy. It was heaven, heaven on earth. Reclaimed glass, stained wood floors. Oh, and the polish sausage, ohmigoodness." Anne drifted off a minute, thinking of the Polish, drizzling with mustard and fried onions. She snapped out of it. "That's all gone now. But there's a Salvage One store there that has everything from Chicago. I remember it was last year when I went there and they had items from a closed firehouse. That's where I got the grenade. I should have bought more but CC rushed me out. We should go." Anne called over to the waitress. "Check."

They paid the check and headed back toward the car. But where it was, it wasn't. Anne's heart raced. "This is where I parked, right, Ingrid?" Anne looked up and down the street, looking for a tow zone sign. She ran up the corner, huffing, looking up the next block. She thought about all her parking tickets, but she would have gotten the boot first before being towed.

"Anne, where's the car?" Ingrid stood, glancing over her shoulder.

"I think it was towed but I don't see any *No Parking* signs."

"Really?"

Anne ran into the middle of the street.

"What are you doing?" Ingrid called to her.

She knelt down and dabbed her finger in the fresh oil stain. "Following the trail." Anne walked a few hundred feet, knelt down and felt the oil stain. This continued for blocks, and then the trail went cold. She opened her phone, stared at her contact list at the little Union Jack flag but she couldn't bring herself to dial the number. She was on her own. She deserved to be on her own. Instead she called 9-1-1.

Chapter Thirteen

CC picked Anne up early Saturday morning. While she drove to their pop-up store, Anne dialed her insurance company. "I can't believe this," she said while on hold. "Who would want a 24-year old car?"

"For parts. Sometimes they're more valuable," CC replied.

"I'm not worried about the car. I'm worried about what was inside it," Anne said. She held her finger up. "Hi, yes, I'm still here," she spoke into the phone. "Yes, Anne Hillstrom, that's right. Mercury Mystique. It was stolen in front of Katrina's Resale on Harlem Avenue. $500 deductible? What about everything inside?" Anne paused, pulling a long sheet of paper out of her pocket. "I'm ready." She read off, "Copper birdbath, 18-pack paper towels, cat litter, dolly, snow shovel, cashmere throw, case of Mason jars. No, I'm not done. In the trunk I had a Hull garden pot, a box of vintage *National Geographics*, three hummingbird feeders—all stained glass, very old, very expensive."

CC listened, wondering just how large the four-door sedan was.

Anne gave the agent the police report number and hung up. In the back seat, Ingrid was sound asleep. CC checked her rearview mirror. "Ingrid," she blurted out.

Ingrid popped up, her eyes wide open. "Ja?"

"What time did you get home last night? I fell asleep on the couch and finally went upstairs around 2 a.m. I knocked on your door."

"Cousin CC, it was very late." Ingrid rolled over on her side and went back to sleep.

In the front seat, Anne smiled a smiley smirk.

"What are you smiling about?" CC asked.

"She didn't tell you about her date?" Anne asked.

"No, she mentioned she was going out. She ran out the door before telling me more than that."

"Maybe I'm speaking out of turn then. Maybe you should ask her." Anne put her phone back in her bag.

CC glanced sideways at Anne. "No, please, be out of turn. Talk to me."

"That nice young attractive, I mean, really hot fireman. His name is Adam, by the way. He asked her out on a date."

"He did, did he? Funny, she didn't mention him after the fire."

"It was kind of last minute. They had been texting and he had a night off. They went bowling."

"Bowling until 2 a.m.?"

"After bowling, they were going to a bar."

"Bar? She's 18. Does he know she's 18?"

"Not a bar, not a real bar. Adam and his buddies are opening a bar, and he wanted to show Ingrid. Here's the good news."

"There's more?" CC asked with a concerned look.

"They want to decorate the bar with vintage firefighter memorabilia and antiques. I already had a couple things which I gave to Ingrid, and we made plans to go to the salvage store for more."

"Really? When did this all happen? Where have I been? You know, Anne, she's my cousin, my family. Why is she telling you everything?"

Anne became quiet, reached for the door handle. "Look, we're here."

Before CC could say anything else, Anne was out the door. CC stepped on the brake and the VW jerked to a stop. Ingrid woke up. The three Spoon Sisters stood outside surveying the damage to the sweet shop next door. The doors and windows had been boarded over with plywood. "Luckily, it was an all-brick building so it didn't spread to the rest of the neighbors," CC said.

Ingrid took a whiff of the cold morning air. "You'd think for a fire in a sweet shop it would smell a little better?"

"All I smell is burnt caramel and mint," Anne said, sniffing the air. "It's the same smell I smelled the night of the fire."

"I don't think our fans will notice," CC said. She rubbed her hands together. "Let's empty out the bus and get organized before the sale."

The three Spoon Sisters unloaded the antiques Anne had agreed to part with and placed them around the store. Anne arranged everything, checked tags, marked a few with *NFS*, meaning *Not for Sale*. "What are you doing?" CC asked. "Everything in here is for sale. That's the point. Everything has to go today. This is the last day for the permit."

Anne pouted and crossed out *NFS* on everything except for one Hitchcock dining room chair. Her mother had had one like it, and it had taken her years to find one at a reasonable price. She pulled it up in front of the tiny picture window at the storefront. In the small 6' x 2' sill, she neatly rearranged the display of Lladro figurines, the china tea service, a hurricane lantern and a stack of books. She pulled the chair close to the sill and sat down to keep watch, looking for the periwinkle blue Bentley and its driver Betsy Buttersworth. She was determined if she had to sell her treasures it would be to fans, not to Buttersworth. "Buttersworth," she mumbled out loud.

She checked her vintage Piaget watch. 8:59 a.m. The line had already formed around the block, people snapping pictures of Anne sitting in the window as though she were one of the Beluga whales at the Shedd Aquarium. *Wait a minute, beluga whales, that's not very nice,* she thought. *I haven't gained that much weight. Do you think that's why Nigel isn't attracted to me? Eight, nine pounds at the most, no more than that. I started my low-carb diet again, daily burn, Jazzercise, well. . .going to start.* She walked over to the counter and grabbed an apple cider donut from the box CC had placed on it. She took a bite and sat back down.

Out front, she could see CC with a clipboard, handing out numbers and making sure everyone was in order before opening the doors. Ingrid walked over and sat on the windowsill, facing Anne, with her small orange Prada bag over her shoulder. "Anne, I've got something for you." She reached inside her bag. She handed her a gold medallion. "This is St. George, the saint for courage. I found it in a little shop in Düsseldorf. A soldier wore it into battle in World War I. I thought since you were going into battle today, it would give you courage." She brushed Anne's long blonde hair off her shoulders and fastened the chain around her neck.

"Thank you," Anne said, kissing Ingrid's cheek. The morning sun silhouetted the beautiful young girl, giving her an ethereal glow. At that moment, Anne thought of her as a guardian angel. Anne turned from the angel to see the devil—Buttersworth—standing in the doorway. She rubbed the medallion, praying for strength, courage.

"Hillstrom," Buttersworth said.

"Buttersworth," was Anne's response.

Buttersworth slammed the door behind her, locking it. "I'm not here for your trinkets, your hand-me-downs. I'm here about Nigel."

"What about Nigel?"

"You know what about Nigel. Inviting him out to dinner behind my back, trying to steal him away from me."

"I did no such thing." Anne jumped up from her chair.

"You know that Nigel has a soft spot for you. He has a Don Quixote complex but you're not his Dulcinea."

"I don't know what you're talking about." Anne walked to the counter.

Betsy grabbed her by her arm and flipped her around. "That's it, Hillstrom. This ends today." She reached in her purse. Ingrid jumped, thinking Betsy was pulling out a gun, but what she pulled out was something much more deadly. Her checkbook. "I'm taking it all."

"You can't have it." Anne stretched her arms out wide, attempting to cover the expanse of the store.

Buttersworth looked past Anne and then ran to the front window. She grabbed the Lladros and smashed them on the floor. She wrote a check, throwing it on the shards. Anne screamed. Betsy ran over to the one-of-a-kind Van Briggle art deco vase on the shelf and tipped it over with her index finger. It smashed into a thousand pieces. She scribbled a check and tossed it on the floor. Ingrid tried to step in.

Anne yelled. "Stand back. This is between me and her."

And, then both their eyes locked on the Flora Danica china that Anne had won at the Lake Forest Rummage Sale. The set that Betsy had willingly given up in a moment of kindness. That moment was long gone. They raced to the hutch where it held a place of prominence—both women's fingertips reaching, stretching. Both bodies were parallel to the floor as they flew into the hutch. The hutch teetered; the set of Flora Danica wobbled. Anne looked up, lying on her back on the floor. She blocked her face as the entire set exploded around her like mortars on a battlefield. Betsy stood over her, looking down, writing checks and throwing them as each piece hit the floor.

CC finally got the front door open and stormed in. "What is going on? Everyone is watching."

Anne looked up and saw all the faces pushed up against the window. Her breath came out in shallow gasps. She didn't even try to count to ten. She muttered, "Buttersworth."

Betsy walked up to CC, signed her name to a blank check and handed it to her. "All the rest is mine." Before leaving, Buttersworth knocked the box of donuts to the floor. "I'll take those too." She left, slamming the door behind her.

Ingrid knelt down next to Anne, who was sobbing. "The waste, the senseless waste."

CC knelt down. "Annie, it's okay; it's okay. She paid for everything."

"It's not the money. I never cared about the money. All these orphaned artifacts could have gone to good homes. Someone who would love them, cherish them like I do. Someone who would care for them. Now there's history shattered all over the floor, erased from existence. Hundreds of years of artisans' memories; craftsmanship faded like a vapor trail, just like their makers."

CC went back outside and apologized to the fans. She explained there would be no sale today. She promised that she would find for each and every single one of them the items they had come for today. She took some selfies with some of them and signed some autographs. She gave hugs. As the crowd dispersed, CC thought she had done pretty good damage control. She was about to go back inside when an old Jeep Cherokee pulled up in front. The last time she'd seen that Jeep was on a dark highway in a Smoky Mountain pass. Its driver, Chief John Blackbear, came up to CC, towering over her. He took her hand in his, shaking it. "CC, so good to see you again."

"Chief Blackbear, what are you doing here?"

"Anne texted me about the cigar store statue she found."

"Oh." CC turned red, thinking of the stereotype.

John Blackbear laughed. "Don't be embarrassed. I was interested in it for my personal collection, for my house. I have a lot of Smoky Mountain artifacts. Good or bad, it is part of our history."

"Of course." She was about to tell him to come in but then glanced through the front door. Anne was curled up on the floor, sobbing. "Give me a minute." She walked into the store, closing the door behind her. "Anne, pull yourself together. John Blackbear is here."

Anne slowed her sobbing. "Bear, John, John Blackbear. He's here?" She sat up, wiped her eyes. "How do I look? Ingrid, hand me my handkerchief and lipstick in my bag."

Anne grabbed both and ran to the back room. She sat at the little office desk, studying her face in the desktop mirror. She cleaned herself up, freshened her lipstick. She pressed her hands down her Diane von Furstenberg wrap dress and went back into the showroom. "Okay, let him in. I'm ready."

CC opened the door; John Blackbear walked in. He unbuttoned his long camel hair overcoat and folded it over his arm. Anne smiled a big smile. She'd forgotten how handsome he was and how big he was. Even through his Armani suit, his muscles rippled as he walked toward her. "Annie, my Annie. You look absolutely beautiful." He bent down and kissed both her cheeks.

Anne reached up and grabbed his lapels, pulling him down and kissing him on his lips. CC grabbed Ingrid. "Let's go for a walk."

Ingrid paused, smiling and watching. CC grabbed her. "Let's go now."

John Blackbear pulled back and looked around the room. "Looks like there's been a little trouble."

"Everything's fine now." Anne heard the tribal drums pounding in her ears. Her hands started to sweat. "Are you in town for long?"

"I came to see the statue and to see you, of course."

"Of course," she said with a wily smile. "Why don't you come in the back room? I'll show you both."

CC and Ingrid walked to the corner coffee shop. They sat down at the counter. The cute young waitress greeted them. "Oh, you're from the antique store down the block. I've seen you out there. I saw the sign. I thought your sale was today."

"We're sold out," CC said.

"That was fast." She poured them both a cup of coffee. "Can I get you anything else? Our specials are a cranberry oatmeal or we have a very nice peppermint glazed French toast."

"Ohmigosh, no, that's all I've been smelling all morning—mint from the fire," CC said.

"Oh, yes, Stella, the sweet shop lady; that was so sad. I'll miss her. Her caramels were my favorite."

"Did she make holiday specials? Like mint? White chocolate?"

The waitress laughed. "Stella? No, she was old school. Just pure caramel. Even the chocolates were very basic. She wasn't very experimental with her flavors, but they were good. I'll miss them."

Ingrid glanced up from the menu. "You know, CC, that's one thing I miss about leaving Germany is the food. This time of year we would be having angel's braid, mom's sour cream yeast bread with brandied soaked almonds, raisins, candied orange peels, or eggs and frankfurters with a green sauce, or my favorite— eggs and mustard sauce."

"Mustard sauce?" The waitress wrinkled her nose, rested her elbows on the counter.

"It's delicious. You know, I could make it for you. I could show you."

"That'd be great. I'm Caitlyn," the waitress said.

"I'm Ingrid."

"You're from Germany?"

"Yes, I'm staying with my cousin, CC, here. I'm going to school."

"Me too. Where are you going?"

"I'm going to Columbia College for creative writing," Ingrid said.

"I go to DePaul," Caitlyn said. "Maybe we can ride the train together."

"That'd be fun."

As they spoke, CC stared into her coffee cup, swirling the cream around, thinking about mint. Ingrid stood up and followed Caitlyn into the kitchen. She grabbed a saucepan and placed a slab of butter in it. Once the butter had melted, she added flour and a bullion cube, bringing it to a boil. She turned to Caitlyn. "The secret is you must stir constantly." Ingrid grabbed some yellow mustard and sugar and cream. She seasoned with salt and pepper. As the sauce simmered, she grabbed some hard-boiled eggs and cut them in half lengthwise. Then she poured the hot mustard sauce over the eggs. "Do you have mashed potatoes?"

"We have hash browns."

"Those will do." Ingrid put the eggs over the hash browns. She took a fork and took a little piece and fed it to Caitlyn.

"When you said mustard, I was turned off. It's really good."

Ingrid carried two plates out, putting one down in front of CC. She sat back down. CC checked the time on her iPhone—twenty minutes since Chief Blackbear had arrived. She went back to her plate. "These are really good, Ingrid. You'll have to give me the recipe."

When they finished their breakfast, they stepped outside. CC looked down the block and saw the Jeep drive off. They walked back to the store. Anne sat in the chair by the window—her hair disheveled, adjusting her dress. CC stared at Anne through the window. It reminded her of the women who posed in picture windows in the red light district in Amsterdam. She was embarrassed to admit this fleeting thought to herself but she giggled anyway.

CC and Ingrid walked into the store. No one said a word. Finally, Anne broke the silence. "Well, John Blackbear did it."

"Excuse me?" CC asked.

"He got what he came for."

"Excuse me?" CC asked again.

Anne smiled. "The cigar store Indian. He bought the Indian."

"I'm glad he left satisfied."

"Yes," Anne said. "Satisfied."

Chapter Fourteen

Feeling rejuvenated, Anne started down the trail of the antique cake knife. Her search began at her favorite used bookstore in downtown Oak Park, The Book Table. Anne loved the touch and smell of paper. She had a Kindle but preferred *real* books. as she called them. Books with a backbone. The section on antiques was large as Oak Park residents were enthusiasts; however, there were only a few books about Parisian antiques. She took the books from the shelf and settled in at a small table in the back. Out of her bag, she pulled out her low-carb snack, trail mix with almonds, and cashews sprinkled with a few chocolate-covered blueberries. Not quite low carb but still good for her. She took a nibble and opened the first book, *Silversmiths of the 1700s*. The first chapter was dated 1790 to 1798. Images of eagles, horseheads, roosters. Nothing close to her fleur de lis. She took the cake knife out of her bag. She opened the book on French silverware from 1750 to 1795. None of the images came close to her cake knife. She was starting to believe it was not as old as she thought it was, but she knew the mark signifying silver was the standard mark for the late 1700s.

The hours faded as the stacks of books in front of Anne grew higher. Anne skimmed through anything she could find about Paris and the late 1700s. When she was about ready to give up, she found one last book on the shelf, entitled *Treasures of Versailles*. On page 198, there was a drawing of her cake knife. What was more exciting was who was holding it—Marie Antoinette. Anne rubbed her eyes to make sure she was seeing what she was seeing. She held the cake knife up. There could be no doubt. The jewel in the drawing was placed exactly where hers was. The ornate carving, even the replica of the mark in the book, was identical.

She read the paragraph, "Marie Antoinette's personal silversmith's mark was the crown and fleur di lis." Underneath it, the caption read, "According to legend, this was the cake knife Marie Antoinette used when she said, 'Let them eat cake.'" Anne slammed the book shut and looked around the tiny back reading room, expecting to see French guards coming to arrest her. She put the knife back in her bag, paid for the book and ran out of the store.

Her heart pounded as she drove her rental car at a devil's pace down Lake Street as she made her way to Glen Ellyn. She burst open the door. She stood in the doorway holding the cake knife in one hand and the book in the other. CC and Ingrid gasped. "What are you doing?" CC yelled.

"Let them eat cake!" she yelled back.

CC and Ingrid looked at each other and then back at Anne. "What?"

Bandit circled around Anne, barking.

"Anne, put the cake knife down." CC got up, pushed Anne into the living room and closed the front door.

"Let them eat cake!" she yelled again.

CC carefully unfolded Anne's grip around the cake knife and placed it on the coffee table in front of the couch. Bandit sniffed it, wiggled his butt and lay back down in the corner, disappointed that there was no cake to be had. "Anne, what are you talking about?"

"This is what we know. This cake knife." Anne reached for it again. "The stone, the green stone in the handle is not glass. I believe it's a real emerald; in fact,

I believe it's almost a flawless emerald, maybe five carats. We know that the cake knife is pure silver by the mark. The silversmith's mark also tells us it's from the late 1700s." Anne opened the book, flipping it around, displaying the drawing of Marie Antoinette holding the cake knife. "The silversmith was Marie Antoinette's personal silversmith. This is the cake knife she used when she said, 'Let them eat cake'."

CC took the book, examined the picture and then checked the title on the spine. "*Treasures of Versailles.* Anne, did you pick up this knife when we were in Versailles? Just to look at it and accidentally put it in your bag?"

"No, of course not. I don't even remember seeing it at Versailles. According to the book, the knife disappeared during the revolution."

"How'd you end up with it?"

"I don't know. That's just the thing. We were in so many tiny shops in Paris, flea markets outside of Paris. You know how these things just turn up. They sit for a hundred years, and then someone finds them in an attic and brings them in to a pawnshop. It happens. You know it happens."

"I don't think we have enough evidence to prove this is Marie Antoinette's knife, but if that emerald is real, I think you're going to make a lot of money from it."

Anne grabbed the knife back and crushed it to her chest. "Oh, no, I'm not selling this."

"Anne, it belongs in a museum."

"You think tourists in their Bermuda shorts and floppy hats are going to appreciate this cake knife as much as me? Is that what you think?"

"Anne." CC sat next to her on the couch and put her hand on top of Anne's. "Let's do some more research. We'll verify it first and then we can talk about what to do with it."

Anne didn't relinquish her grip on the cake knife.

"I've been thinking all day about something," CC said, changing the subject.

"The cake knife?"

"No, Anne, not the cake knife. I've been thinking about mint."

Anne gave CC a confused glance.

"Mint, Anne. The morning of the fire you said you could smell caramel and mint."

"Yes?" Anne said.

"When I spoke to Caitlyn, a waitress at the diner, she told me that Stella, the sweet shop lady, would never mix mint with caramel."

"So?"

"That's just the thing. You said that you smelled caramel and mint before you saw the smoke."

"And?"

"What I'm saying is that I think we need to check the mixing vat to see why you smelled mint and caramel."

"How do we do that?"

"Ingrid and I've already made arrangements." CC walked over to the small hall closet and pulled out a crowbar. "Let's go."

By the time they reached the sweet shop, the street was empty and dark. The light snow glistened in the headlights of the VW bus. They drove around to the back to the small alley behind the store that the sweet shop shared with their pop-up store. CC led the way. Anne swiveled her head back and forth, keeping an eye out. CC pried off the plywood covering the door window. She reached inside and unlocked the door. The strong smell of mint and burnt caramel assaulted them. Anne covered her nose. "That's it. That's the vat where I found Stella. She was hunched over buried up to the waist in caramel." Anne pointed at the large stainless steel mixing vat.

CC examined the mixing blades, running her hand up along the shaft that attached to the motor. She took a sniff. "Stella's body jammed the blade, causing the motor to burn out." CC walked along the burnt walls, examining the shredded wires. "These wires are encased in cloth. This is the original electrical for this building, maybe 80 years old." CC reached into the vat.

"What are you doing?" Anne asked.

CC pulled up a gallon jug of mint extract, empty and dented. She shined her flashlight on the shaft of the mixing vat that was covered with caramel. She looked at the caramel in the bowl which only went halfway up the vat. "How did the shaft get covered in caramel?"

"Maybe she dropped the mint extract jug in accidentally, reached in to grab it and got stuck by the blade," Anne said. "That caused the caramel to splash."

"If she was struck by the blade, it wouldn't have splashed." CC reached up and grabbed the shaft with her sticky hand as though someone was holding her down. "Look." CC shined the light on the shaft. She stuck her face down into the vat.

"What are you doing?" Anne asked.

"Just wait." CC reached up with her right hand and grabbed the shaft. She shined her light where her hand was at the beginning of the sticky caramel residue. "The shaft is dry up until this point. The length of an average size right arm. Stella was right handed. I noticed that when we met her. I also noticed she had unusually big hands. Much larger than mine. Look, the caramel goes all the way around the shaft as though she was hanging onto it for dear life."

"What are you saying?"

"I'm saying that somebody held Stella's head down in the caramel. Stella was murdered."

Chapter Fifteen

Glen Ellyn Police Detective Rick Phillips stared at CC. He nodded politely as she spoke. She could tell he was only half-listening. CC gave her theory about the caramel on the shaft. When they were done, the detective smiled and opened a file folder sitting in front of him on his desk. "It's a very interesting story. And how did you get into the store, ma'am?"

Anne and CC looked at each other. Before they could answer, Phillips closed the file. "Her death is under investigation. Thank you for coming in."

"That's it?" CC asked. "That's all you're going to say?"

He smiled. "It's an ongoing investigation."

"Do you know who we are?" Anne asked.

The police detective said, "Yes, I'm aware of your blog."

"Then why won't you believe us?"

"Miss Hillstrom, the Glen Ellyn police prefer to conduct their own investigations. As much as we appreciate private citizens sticking their noses into our business, breaking into private buildings is a crime. I suggest you leave the investigation to the police and mind your own store. I think we're done here."

Anne stood up in a huff. She stormed out followed by CC. "Of all the——. I can't believe it."

"Maybe he's right. Maybe we've overstepped our boundaries," CC said. "It's just that I have a hard time letting things go."

"Are you doubting yourself now? Do you think it's possible that it *was* an accident?" Anne asked.

CC had nothing to say. The girls walked the few blocks to their small storefront. They stood inside, surveying the devastation that Betsy had caused. Ingrid was sweeping up the shards of glass, crystal and china. "What did the police say?" Ingrid asked.

"They didn't believe us," Anne said. She flopped down on the ornate gold and red velvet couch that hadn't been sold yet, rubbing her hands on the plush velvet. "I can't believe I'm letting Buttersworth have this."

"Ms. Buttersworth called. She made arrangements for movers to pick everything up tomorrow," Ingrid said.

"At least you made enough money to hold you over until the bank straightens things out," CC said.

Anne counted the money in her head. There was a pink Limoges plate she'd been watching on eBay. It was time to rebuild her empire. That would be her first purchase before she paid her mortgage. She needed to fill the void that Buttersworth was leaving in her wake. She needed to feel good about herself again. She had lost everything. Her money, her antiques, Nigel.

Ingrid sat down next to Anne, putting her arm around her. "I know you're going to miss all these wonderful things. It must have been so hard for you to sell them. Caitlin told me about an indoor flea market at the DuPage County Fairgrounds. Perhaps we can go there and you can continue teaching me?"

A small smile grew on Anne's face. Ingrid watered it. She nudged her, giving her an encouraging look. The smile grew larger. CC came over. "What are you two talking about?"

"Nothing." Anne replied.

When CC had gone into the back room, Anne said, "Let's keep this between you and me. I'll pick you up on the corner."

Ingrid smiled and gave Anne a kiss on the cheek. She returned to sweeping the shattered remains.

Chapter Sixteen

Anne munched on her bag of kettle corn. She hadn't been able to resist the smell of the freshly popped corn. It emanated throughout the crowded exhibit hall. The flea market was held in the largest building on the fairgrounds, which spanned a large expanse adjacent to the DuPage County Courthouse and Jail. Dealers were spread throughout the building, a mixture of primitives, textiles, smalls and furniture.

Anne had already stopped Ingrid from purchasing a knock-off Hermes scarf. In her quest for popcorn, she'd lost track of Ingrid. She glanced around, searching for the tall blonde. She spotted her in the corner. Two men at a booth were flirting with her. Anne approached them, grabbing Ingrid by the elbow and pulling her away.

Out of the corner of her eye, Anne saw something green hanging from a wooden rafter. She went over to it and tried to touch it. It was out of her reach. Its green slag glass was encased in its original brass flowered scroll work. She'd been looking for a lantern like this for her bathroom. It was in excellent condition, no chips, breaks or missing parts. "Can you tell me about this lamp?" she asked the dealer who was sitting on a chair, eating a sandwich. The woman got up and came over by the lamp.

"That's an original piece from 1910. My husband got it from an old hotel in Woodstock that was being torn down."

"It's beautiful," Anne said. "Can you do a little better on the price?"

The woman negotiated with Anne. They settled on an amount. Anne reached into her bag and pulled out a wad of hundred dollar bills. She'd cashed Betsy's check and allowed herself a little fun money for today. In fact, she'd brought all the proceeds from the sale just in case. She decided she wouldn't leave tonight until she'd spent every dime. It was ill-gotten gain coming from Buttersworth. Anne would have nothing to do with it except to spend it.

"I'll take this, too." Anne pointed to a tapestry-sewing basket. "And this." She picked up an early copy of *Gone with the Wind*. "Can you hold this for me?" Anne made arrangements to pick up the lamp on her way out.

A crowd was gathering in a nearby booth. Anne went to see what the commotion was about. Ingrid was standing in the center of the crowd, holding up a cuckoo clock. "This is in the style of the Black Forest cuckoo clock makers. More specifically, Herzlich Willkommen. He still makes cuckoo clocks in the Black Forest. This is why I know this is not an antique cuckoo clock. This one is hand carved. It's from the Black Forest but it's certainly not over a hundred years old, the reason being is that pre-World War II cuckoo clocks are very valuable. The Black Forest was depleted of its lumber during the war. For many years Black Forest cuckoo clocks were not made and many of the clocks made after World War II were carved from new-growth trees that were planted after the war and not the 300-year-old trees. You can tell the difference by looking at the grain of the wood." Ingrid held it up. "See, in this clock, it's a young tree. If you look close enough you can count the lines in the wood on the back or the bottom of the clock which shows the age of the tree. Also, the wood doesn't have the same deep rich patina of the pre-war clocks. This one has been stained to replicate that deep walnut color. It's a very nice replica."

Anne was mesmerized. Her student had become a teacher. It was a proud moment for her. She clapped, which inspired the crowd to join her. Ingrid smiled and put the cuckoo clock back on the table in front of the angry dealer. Anne was jostled as someone bumped into her. Anne felt a quick tug. It took her a moment to realize that her bag, *the* large orange Prada bag, was no longer on her shoulder. She stood still for a moment, as the vacuum of realization closed in around her like a plastic bag over her head. She couldn't breath. Then she scanned the crowd. She caught a glimpse of orange running out the front door. She ran, followed by Ingrid. "Anne, what's wrong?"

Anne turned her head back over her shoulder, huffing. "My purse. My cake knife," she gasped out in between heavy breaths.

Ingrid followed her out into the dark parking lot. One overhead streetlamp flickered. Anne stopped, bent over, catching her breath. "What happened?" Ingrid said.

"Somebody grabbed my bag."

"Which way did he run?"

Anne looked at the three outbuildings, long barrack-like steel structures. From the last, they could see its front door closing. They ran across the parking lot over the open field. Anne stumbled on the uneven, snow-covered ground. She recovered, limping but still running. Ingrid made it into the building first. Anne followed, gasping for air.

Ingrid turned on her iPhone flashlight, shining it around the dark building. The building was full of hay and pens for the livestock. Ingrid shined her light on the floor, bent down, and picked something up. She turned with a tear in her eye, holding up a piece of the large orange Prada bag handle, severed from its body. Anne screamed. It was her worst nightmare. They walked down the center aisle, shining their light into all the pens. When they reached the end of the building, they saw the deflated bag, missing a limb. Anne picked it up, checked inside. It was empty. She took the piece of the cut handle and placed it on its nub. A deep rage was brewing inside her. She grabbed a pitchfork lying against the wall. They walked down the next aisle. Then they heard footsteps behind them.

Ingrid dropped her phone. The room went pitch dark. Anne readied her pitchfork. Ingrid held onto her arm. A shadow walked towards them in the darkness, the hay rustling under its feet. Anne tried to make out the figure. Her eyes were still adjusting to the dark. She jabbed forward with the pitchfork. They heard a scream and then the shadow ran off and out the door. The door slammed behind it. Ingrid found her phone on the floor and turned on the flashlight. She saw Anne posed like a bayonetting soldier, the tip of the pitchfork dripping with blood. Anne dropped the pitchfork. On the ground, she made out her pewter salt and peppershakers, her Hermes scarf and the cake knife. She picked up her treasures, clinging to them. "Let's get out of here," she said to Ingrid.

Chapter Seventeen

Anne sat on CC's couch and held up her wounded orange Prada bag. "He cut it right off my shoulder. Ingrid and I chased him across the open field into the animal stalls."

"That's terrifying," CC interrupted, bringing cups of tea for everyone.

"Anne stuck him good with a pitchfork. We found blood all over the hay," Ingrid interjected, her blue eyes wide and excited.

"Did you see his face?"

They both shook their heads.

"Thank goodness, he dropped the cake knife."

"Do you think he knew what you were carrying in the bag?"

"He had to. Why me? Out of a thousand people at the flea market? Why me?"

"You were buying quite a bit. I saw you at one booth waving a fistful of hundred dollar bills," Ingrid said.

"Anne!" CC exclaimed.

"It's my share of the Buttersworth money. I wanted to replenish our stock."

"The point was to sell out, which we did. Now we'll have to start over again. How are you going to pay your bills?" CC asked.

"The bank's working on it," Anne said with a false confidence.

"If the cake knife is as valuable as you think it is, I think you need to sell it," CC said.

Anne pulled it out of her damaged bag, held it up to the light. "I risked my life for this knife. There's no way I'm selling it."

"We need to authenticate it and we need to find out where you bought it and who wants it," CC said.

Anne let Sassy out of her carrier before she flopped back down on the couch. Bandit chased Sassy under the dining table. She hissed at him. Bandit wiggled his tailless butt in appreciation. Anne took off her shoes and rubbed her feet. Ingrid sat next to her and did the same. "CC, I've gone through all my receipts. I've gone through my notebooks with every purchase. I can find no record of buying this cake knife. That's what's bothering me."

"Okay, Anne, first thing we do is retrace all our steps. I'll make another pot of tea. This might take a while." CC looked around her kitchen for the perfect teapot for the situation. She chose her Arabia Finland teapot by Ulla Procope, a vintage 1960s ceramic with its twisted bamboo handle. She steeped some Earl Grey. As the teapot simmered, she ran to the pantry to find a treat to accompany the tea. She grabbed the tin of shortbread cookies that she had made earlier in the day. As she waited for the pot to boil, she realized for the first time how excited she was. There was nothing she liked better than unraveling a mystery. There was a problem to be solved, and she would solve it. Her entire career as a journalist prepared her to search for answers. The first step would be to ask the right questions. The teapot howled. She put the tea in to seep. She carried the tray with the tea, teacups and shortbread into the living room.

The snow had begun again. CC felt a chill—a chill of excitement and a chill of Chicago winter. She threw an oak log into the fireplace along with some apple wood kindling from her fall garden. As the fire took, the smell of oak and apple wood filled the room. The three Spoon Sisters pulled the matching gray mid-century Ceni armchairs closer to the fire and settled in for a long night. Anne sipped her tea and nibbled on her shortbread cookie. Bandit waited patiently for any mishap, any slip of a hand, any drop of a cookie. Ingrid closed her eyes. She felt like a character in a cozy mystery surrounded by her mentors. She had read about their adventures and now she was living in one.

"Anne, I recall almost all of the sales that we went to together in Paris," CC said. "And I don't recall you buying the cake knife. I would have. It's not to say you couldn't have bought it and threw it into your purse when I was looking around. I just think at some point you would have shown it to me."

"Yes, Yes, I would have. And if I had it in my purse, don't you think I would have been stopped at security before we boarded the plane in France? It's not sharp. It's a rounded point, but technically it is a weapon."

"You did set off the alarms. I remember them taking out your pewter salt and pepper shakers, your bookmark, your pen collection but I don't remember the knife."

"And I carried my orange Prada bag onto the plane. I held it the whole. . ." Anne paused. "The turbulence! When the plane dropped and the lights went out, I dropped my bag on the floor. The man next to me—you know, the poor fellow who died, Bernie—he dropped his bag too and he was in a horrible panic. The flight attendant came over to calm him down. He kept reaching for his bag but they wouldn't let us unbuckle our seat belts. The flight attendant picked up both our bags. . . . It was *his* knife." She paused as realization struck her. "He must have been smuggling it out of France and somebody on the plane *killed* him for it. Now they're after *me*. Oh, my goodness!" She put the knife back in her purse. "I've been looking for my change purse. The one with the gold beading. I thought I'd left it in the hotel room but I bet you it fell out on the plane. I have a little note card inside it that says, 'If found, return to Anne Hillstrom with my cell number.' That's how they found me! What do we do?"

The fire died down as Anne's cell phone rang. All three girls gasped. It rang again. "Well, answer it," CC urged.

"I don't want to answer it."

It rang a third time.

Anne opened up the phone cover to see the Union Jack. She gave a relieved glance to CC and Ingrid. "It's Nigel." She hit the red *decline* button. "I don't want to talk to him."

It rang again. She hit *decline* again. Her text alert beeped. "It's Nigel," Anne read out loud, "The sweet shop lady was murdered. Call me now." She dialed Nigel back and put him on speakerphone. "Nigel, you're on speaker with CC and Ingrid."

"Hello, ladies," he said in his most charming Liverpudlian accent.

Anne missed that accent.

"Anne, the sweet shop lady was murdered."

"Yes, we know. CC figured it out. We're the ones who told the police."

"Yes, but I have new information," he said.

Anne tapped her foot. She was losing patience. She kept picturing Nigel at dinner with Buttersworth. She fought hard not to hang up.

"Listen, Anne, the Glen Ellyn police checked one of the red light cameras. Right on the corner by your store. One of the red light officers noticed something."

Anne interrupted, "We're all holding our breath."

"A dark figure was standing in the doorway of your shop and the sweet shop lady was watching him from the sidewalk."

"And?"

"And that was ten minutes before you arrived and found the sweet shop on fire."

Anne became quiet. "Nigel," she said in a soft, tender voice. "Do you think that he's the man who killed the sweet shop lady?"

Silence and then Nigel said, "Yes."

"Nigel," Anne said in a softer, even more tender voice. "Do you think he intended to break into our store?"

Nigel cleared his throat, before saying, "Yes, Anne."

This time Anne barely whispered, "Nigel, could you come over?"

"Yes, Anne."

Anne hung up the phone. "It's my fault the sweet shop lady was killed. He must have been after the cake knife. If I'd have arrived at the store ten minutes earlier, that would have been me. "

"We don't know that," CC said.

"Nigel knows that. I know that," Anne said. Ingrid nodded in agreement.

CC walked over and threw some more apple wood branches on the fire, tapping at it with the poker. "We need to find out who the passenger next to you, who Bernie was," CC said. She glanced at Ingrid whose face was lit up by the glow from her iPhone. "Ingrid, what are you doing?"

"It's Adam. He's been texting me all night."

"Really, now?"

"After all we've been through?" Anne asked.

Ingrid put her phone down.

"You know, Anne," CC began, "O'Hare Airport has a very interesting history. After World War II started, the Army Air Corps was looking for a site in Chicago to build their Douglas C-54 Skymaster transport aircraft. The army settled on Orchard Place, which is the current site of the airport. It began as a factory with four runways constructed to test the planes."

"That's very interesting, CC. What does that have to do with anything?" Anne interrupted CC, while she nibbled on her fourth shortbread cookie.

"I'm getting to it, Anne. Chicago hired engineer Ralph H. Burke, the man who designed Meigs Field and the Chicago subway, to design the master plan. Because of the war effort, steel was at a high demand, but the Civil Aeronautics Association and the state of Illinois made commitments to Orchard Airport. Because of the nearby Gary steel mills and the availability of U.S. steel and the power of Chicago politics, Mayor Kennelly pushed the airport through, naming it after Edward 'Butch' O'Hare, a naval aviator."

"And?"

"Well, I did a story about the Gary steel mills and the steel used to construct O'Hare and the planes. During my research, I met the head of O'Hare security and risk assessment Gregg Ludicki. Gregg evaluates risks for flights and also trains TSA and customs agents. He gave me clearance to access secure areas for my story. Gregg also happens to be a fan of our blog."

As the fire began to smolder, both Anne and Ingrid yawned. "You two have been through a lot tonight," CC said. Bandit chased Sassy across the room. "Bad Bandit," CC said. "She's going to be a momma. Be nice."

Sassy looked at Bandit with her sparkling blue eyes. She seemed to have a glow about her. She tilted her head lovingly and then smacked him across the nose.

Chapter Eighteen

"Okay, Bandit, act natural, like nothing's happening. You're the head of your class and you're certified." The Aussie dog stared back up at CC, not quite understanding what she was saying, but loving the attention anyway. His butt wiggled. They stood in the lobby of the administrative building at O'Hare Field. Gregg Ludicki had agreed to meet with CC.

CC had dressed for the occasion. She took off her long wool coat. Underneath it, she was wearing her favorite black skirt and cashmere sweater. She adjusted herself, top and bottom and fixed her lipstick. It had been years since she'd interviewed Gregg and had drinks with him the day after. At the time, she was still getting over her divorce and wasn't ready for anything more than drinks. But a lot of time and romance had passed since then. She hoped Gregg hadn't changed much.

Bandit scratched at his emotional therapy dog tag. Since the annoying little Chihuahua on the plane, CC was determined to show the world what a real emotional therapy dog looked like. Bandit was happy to oblige, never wanting to be home alone. He sat quietly, sniffing people as they walked by. CC had been very proud of Bandit when he was in training. He'd ignored the long-haired corgi/aussie mix at therapy school. With his purebred bloodline, she knew he was appalled by such an abomination. He managed to work through it, letting out a long, low growl signifying his contempt. Now a handsome pilot walked by and knelt down to pet

Bandit after looking at CC for approval. It'd been almost six months since Nashville and Brent, and years since Tony. She didn't bother thinking about how long it had been since her ex-husband because that was a blessing. Either way, she was ready to date again.

She recognized Gregg immediately. She knelt down next to Bandit and whispered, "He still looks pretty good, Boo Boo." Bandit gave her a kiss on the cheek. Gregg came up and hesitated, shaking her hand and then gave her a hug.

"CC, I'm so happy to hear from you. It's been what? Six or seven years?"

"Yeah, Gregg, about seven years since the article and Smiler Coogan's."

"That was a fun night."

"Yeah."

He looked down at Bandit. "Bandit, right?" He gave her a confused look.

"He's in training to be an emotional support dog."

"For you?"

"Oh heavens, no. I don't need emotional support. I'm training him as an emotional support dog for emotional support dogs."

"I don't understand."

"It turns out that emotional support dogs can get pretty stressed out. They feel their owner's anxiety and having another calming supportive dog around them eases their anxiety. It's the same theory as pairing a thoroughbred horse with a goat in the stall. It calms them down."

At that moment, a poodle was being wheeled by in a carrier. Bandit jumped, strained at his leash, started barking. "Quiet, Bandit." Bandit let out one last bark before lying back down. "Well, he's still in training," CC said.

"Let's go back to my office." The three walked up the stairs to the second floor which overlooked the first floor. Several glass front offices lined the walkway, the third door read *Gregg Ludicki, Head of Security and Risk Assessment*. He held the door open for CC and Bandit. He sat down at his desk.

CC sat across from him and Bandit lay on the floor. "Gregg, I could use your help with something."

"A story you're working on?" Gregg picked up a business card, sliding it through his fingers.

"Something like that."

"Please, go ahead."

"My friend, Anne Hillstrom and I . . . ."

"Of course, the other Spoon Sister," he interrupted.

"Yes, I forgot for a moment that you're a fan."

"Yeah, big fan." Gregg pointed over his shoulder to a shelf full of Chicago Cubs memorabilia, baseballs, bats, and autographed 8 x 10s of Mr. Cub himself— Ernie Banks. "I've written a couple times for advice on locating Cubs memorabilia."

"That's right, I remember." CC crossed her legs, straightening her skirt slightly above her knee. "As I'm sure you're aware, a passenger died on our return flight on our recent trip from Paris."

"Yes, I have that file." He glanced through the pile of manila folders on his desk.

"Well, that passenger was sitting next to Anne. As you can imagine, she's quite upset and is wondering what happened to him."

Gregg tapped on his desk and opened the bottom file drawer. He pulled out a manila file folder. "Some of this is public record, some isn't." He walked over to the glass window and shut the blinds. He sat back down at his desk, opened the file. Inside was a picture of Bernie clipped to it.

As CC stretched her neck over the table, Gregg sat back in his chair and tapped his fingers on the desk. CC flipped her brown hair over her shoulder. She remembered that Gregg had complimented her on her hair the last time they'd met. Gregg began, "His name was Bernie Gladstone, 58, single. He was from Atlanta. According to the coroner's report, he died of blunt trauma to the head. He hit his head on the counter of the lavatory sink."

"Did he have any next of kin?"

"Actually we couldn't find anyone to contact. He had no immediate family and apparently not a lot of friends. We're holding his checked bags in storage."

"What did he do for a living?"

"He had an import/export company," Gregg said.

"What kind of importing?"

"We went through his suitcases and there were samples of French perfume bottles."

Not the news CC had expected.

"Why so many questions?" Gregg asked.

"Anne sat next to a dead body for six hours. You can imagine she was pretty distraught, still is," CC said. "I guess I want to find some closure for her."

"I can tell you there's not much closure. I've seen my share of dead bodies coming off planes. Some heart attacks, some old age and some, like in Bernie's case, accidents." Gregg closed the folder and put it back in his desk drawer. "How about a drink?"

"I don't have a lot of time." CC glanced at her watch.

Gregg opened his other drawer and pulled out a bottle of Jack Daniel's and two shot glasses.

CC nodded. "Just one, one quick shot."

As Gregg poured, he said, "Remember the upside down margaritas at Smiler Coogan's?"

CC downed the shot and inhaled a sharp breath. She felt the burning sensation down her throat. "Yes, I do remember that much from that night, at least."

Gregg laughed. "We both got pretty drunk. You were getting out of a bad marriage at that time, right?" He filled her shot glass, handing it back to her.

Thinking about her marriage, CC decided to accept the shot. She downed it, this one went down much easier.

He filled the third glass as he spoke, "I'm done here if you want to grab dinner. Are you hungry?"

CC downed the fourth shot. "I could eat."

"What about Bandit?"

"We could stop and drop Bandit off. Or, better yet, why don't I make us dinner?"

Gregg stood up, grabbed his jacket off the coat rack. "Let's go."

Bandit jumped up. CC grabbed the edge of the desk and wobbled a little bit, restraining her giggles. "Okay, you drive, Gregg," she said with a laugh.

CC stumbled, landing against Gregg as he opened the passenger door of the black Porsche 911. "This is nice. Is this new?" CC asked.

"I picked it up last week." He closed the door behind her and Bandit.

CC breathed in the new car leather smell, admiring the elegant yet functional design of the German sports car. When he started the engine, *Back in the Saddle* by Aerosmith blasted out of the speakers. CC bobbed her head. Bandit moaned. CC struggled with her seat belt. Gregg reached over, putting his hands around her waist. He clicked the belt and let his hands linger. CC smiled.

A short while later, CC stumbled with her key, trying to unlock her front door. Bandit and Gregg watched patiently, both expecting a treat when they got inside. She dropped the key and laughed. "Let me help you with that," Gregg said, reaching over, picking up the keys and unlocking the door.

CC flipped on the light switch and threw her purse on the entryway table. "Gregg, why don't you have a seat on the couch? I'll see what I have in the fridge."

"Do you have anything to drink?"

"Of course." CC slipped off her heels and ran down to the cellar. She skimmed along her wine rack until she found one of her homemade cherry wines. She checked the date. It was her oldest bottle. Probably her best year. *Appropriate,* she thought. She ran back upstairs and poured them both a glass. She handed one to Gregg and clinked her glass against his.

"This is very good," he said.

"Thank you; the cherries are from my garden. I make my own wine."

Gregg finished his glass. CC looked surprised and went into the kitchen. Carrying the bottle of wine, she came back into the living room. She refilled his glass and sat next to him on the couch. She took a sip of her wine. Her head was starting to spin. It had been a long time, maybe since college, since she drank so many shots. Bandit lay near her feet, keeping a watchful eye.

Gregg finished his glass, reached behind CC, placing it on the console table behind the couch, leaving his arm draped over her shoulder. CC felt a bit nervous and a bit foolish. She barely knew this man. Gregg leaned in, trying to kiss her on the lips. CC turned her head quickly, his lips grazing her cheek. "I better find us something for dinner. What do you think?" She stood up.

Gregg grabbed her hand, pulling her back on the couch next to him. "I'm not hungry." He leaned in again. This time connecting with CC's lips. Bandit let out a low growl.

CC pulled back again and sat quiet. She was having second thoughts. Maybe this wasn't such a good idea. Her head ached. "Hey, Gregg, I'm sorry but I'm really tired. Maybe we should call it a night."

He put his arm around her again. "That's what you said at Smiler Coogan's that night. I thought we'd hit it off."

"Yeah, I had a good time, and it was nice seeing you again. It's just I'm really tired. I think we should call it a night."

"I'm not ready to leave yet," he said.

She pushed back at him and stood up. "I'd like you to leave right now." Bandit stood up.

Gregg glanced at Bandit, who was staring him down. "Hey, I'm sorry. I had a little too much to drink. Let's make it another time." He stood up.

"Sure, that'd be good," CC said. She walked him to the door and locked it behind him. Bandit walked over and circled around her several times. He lay down at her feet while CC looked out the door window making sure Gregg left. She knelt down and hugged Bandit, kissing his nose. "What a good boy you are."

Chapter Nineteen

Anne balanced the collection of bags she'd gathered at the early bird estate sale. After finding a stray $20 bill crammed into her coat pocket, she'd waited in line for over an hour to be among the first to enter. It was all business. Everything she'd bought was for one of their fans. She felt that she'd let them down. Buttersworth had gotten her grubby little hands on everything. She walked past her two-car garage, staring at the door, knowing what was behind it and what she'd have to do. Not just for the money to pay bills but for her fans. She thought about the little girl, Dakota, she'd met at the first sale and how her eyes lit up when Anne gave her the doll. She thought about another fan named Ida and a Steiff bear she'd found her. Yes, this was the right thing to do. This is what Great Aunt Sybil would have wanted, placing orphaned artifacts in good homes. She let out a deep sigh. With her shoulders slumped over, she went up the back stairs to her enclosed porch.

"Miss Hillstrom."

Anne jumped, dropping her bags. A figure stood up from inside her porch.

"I hope you don't mind me waiting for you."

Anne took a step back as he came out of the porch. "Oh, Professor Gildwin. What are you doing here?"

He smiled. "I see I've upset you. I'm sorry. I was sitting in my car for a few hours and got out to stretch my legs. I thought maybe I'd missed you so I tried knocking on the door."

Anne stared at him. "What do you want?"

"Please can we sit down? Do you have a minute?"

They went back into the porch. Anne sat down in the white wicker rocking chair, hugging her bags. He sat on the chair across from her. "I've sent several emails to your partner, CC, about the drawing desk. I came today to see if I could buy it from you. I'll give you $500 cash."

"Professor, I appreciate your offer, and I also appreciate the fact that you made us aware of the art school closing. CC and I try the best we can to fill requests for our fans. As I told you, I have some paintings and supplies, some of them very old, from the school, but the desk I'm saving for CC. You see, she's a bit of an artist. You might have seen pictures of her work on her blog."

The professor smiled. "Yes, I did see them."

"I think the desk will be a perfect Christmas gift for her."

"I understand your reluctance to sell it. Can I at least see it? I saw the pictures on the blog but I'd love to see it in person. It ties into my research." He paused. "I'm working on a book about mid to late neo-impressionists and many of the artists were associated with the school as teachers or students. Because they didn't embrace impressionism, they were considered revolutionists."

"Oh, certainly, that's the least I can do." She stood up. "It's in the garage."

They walked down the stairs. Anne opened the large overhead door. The desk was in front where Ingrid had placed it. The professor immediately looked over the desk, running his hand along the edges. "This is definitely authentic. This would be the type of drawing desk they would have used. It's really wonderful to touch history."

"Yes, exactly," Anne replied, knowing exactly how he felt. "Maybe you can help me. I found these initials

J.C.T. on the desk and I couldn't find any famous painters at that time with those initials."

He studied the initials carved into the wood. "Off hand, I can't think of anyone. It was probably a student doodling. To be honest with you, I find students in my class who tend to drift and doodle. Now we call it ADD. May I?" the professor asked.

Anne nodded.

He flipped the tabletop over. He examined the scratches.

"Oh, this is really neat. Let me show you. You have to step back about ten feet," Anne said. She flipped the underside of the desktop perpendicular.

The professor stood staring, with his finger on his chin. "I see it. I see it now. Somebody scribbled *Sunday in the Park.*" He walked a foot to the left and then stepped a foot to the right. "It seems very good for a student." He came back to Anne. "I wouldn't change a thing on it. Leave it exactly as it is. At first, I wanted it for my study, but now I think it would be perfect in my classroom. I occasionally teach art appreciation at the Art Institute. I would welcome you and CC to come give a talk about the art school and some of the items you found."

Anne beamed. "Oh, CC would love to speak at the Art Institute. She would be so excited."

"Maybe we can make a deal after all for the desk and we can have CC give a talk."

Anne shook the professor's hand. "Give me a couple days to think about it."

"Here's my card with my contact information, including my cell phone." He gave her his business card, turned on his heel and left.

A short while later, CC and Ingrid came by the garage where Anne was sorting through her collection. CC was sipping on a Starbuck's coffee rubbing her temples and wearing dark sunglasses. "Hi, girls." Anne waved at them. "I was sorting through. . ."

CC appeared surprised. "What are you doing?"

"All the money we made from the pop-up sale is gone," Anne said, not looking at CC.

"Anne, that was supposed to be for bills."

"I took a little with me to the flea market. I had to replenish stock, and I lost the rest when my purse was stolen."

"Oh, Anne." CC rubbed her head.

"CC, I know. I'm trying to do the right thing now. I'm trying to find things that I can part with. Let's go through the fan list to see if we can match items with homes. Okay?"

CC nodded her head.

"What's with the sunglasses?" Anne asked.

"My eyes hurt. I have a bit of a headache."

"That's too bad, CC."

"Have you changed your mind about the drawing desk?" Ingrid asked.

"Oh, the drawing desk. You just missed Professor Gildwin. He stopped by to see it. And you're going to love this, CC," Anne said loudly. CC winced. "He said he might have you come give a talk at the Art Institute. He teaches there occasionally."

CC tipped her 1980's Ray-Ban Wayfarers to the tip of her nose and looked over the top. "Really? The Art Institute?"

"Yes, the professor is writing a book on neo-impressionism and he thought it would be interesting for his class to hear about some of the items we bought at the art school sale."

"Did you show him the drawing under the top?" Ingrid asked. "Did you ask him about the initials?"

Before Anne could answer, CC interrupted, "What drawing?"

Ingrid ran over and flipped the desktop over. CC took a few steps and then Anne pushed her a little further back. CC took her sunglasses off, staring at the etching. "Wow, that's a great copy done in pointillism."

"Isn't it?" Anne stood next to CC, admiring the scratches.

CC went up closer to study the drawing, and it disappeared. She ran her hand over the top feeling the thousands of little indents. "It's like Braille. How could you sit at this desk and know what you were drawing? Anne, this is really interesting. What did the professor say?"

"He thought that the drawing was very good but that it was done by a student and those are his initials."

"Even though the artist was a student, it's still a piece of history. We better research the desk and the art school. We should know what we're talking about if we are going to lecture at the Art Institute. Let's start with trying to get a list of registered students." CC studied the etching on the desk. "Anne, you know you don't have to sell all these things."

"Don't say it."

"If the cake knife is authentic, it's worth more than everything in your garage."

"CC, there has to be a limit to what I can give up. That cake knife is one of a kind."

"We don't really know that, do we?"

"It's a spitting image of the one in the book."

"We should at least get the emerald appraised."

"Ohmigosh, you want to sell the emerald and pull it out of this beautiful cake knife?"

"No, of course not."

Anne reached into her large orange Prada bag with the newly sewn on handle. She pulled the cake knife out. The silver blade glistened in the sun, reflecting onto the snow. Ingrid reached into her small orange

Prada bag, pulled out her iPhone and took a selfie with Anne and the cake knife.

"Since I left Ebbort labs, I don't have access to the chemistry lab, but I might be able to convince Sharon to let me in at lunchtime." Anne paused for a moment before opening the trunk of her rental car. It was packed with plastic bags and baubles wrapped in newspaper. "Ingrid, I almost forgot." She pulled out a package wrapped in old newspaper. It was a brass whistle with CFD engraved on it. "Ingrid, this is a Chicago antique firefighter whistle from around the time of the Colombian Exposition." She unwrapped another item. "This is a vintage 1950s metal fire hose cover from a fire truck."

"Where'd you find these things?" CC interrupted.

"This morning. I ran to an estate sale at the house of a former Chicago firefighter. Since Ingrid told me about Adam and the bar, I've been scanning the listings." She reached back into the trunk and pulled something else out. "Look, this is a hanging fire bucket that went on the old wagons. It's a start. I was thinking we could go over to the firehouse, give these to Adam and find out what else he's looking for. What do you think?"

Ingrid smiled. "He's there now. Could we go?"

CC rubbed her temples. "Sure, why not."

When they arrived, Adam was waiting outside the brick firehouse. Ingrid jumped out of the car, ran up and kissed his cheek. He hugged her. Anne followed, carrying the shopping bag with her finds. CC dragged behind. "Come on in. I want to see what you brought." Adam led the way into the firehouse. As they walked to the break room, Anne and CC's heads swayed back and forth scanning all the fireman in their t-shirts and jeans, working on trucks, winding up hoses. Anne stopped dead in her tracks, CC bumping into her back. "CC," Anne whispered.

"I know. Let's keep going."

They entered the break room which had a long farmhouse table. A firefighter was hunched over a big pot at the stove, CC could smell the chili and the fresh-baked cornbread. She was actually feeling better. The chili smelled good, but it was missing something. She reached into her purse and felt her little vial of ghost pepper seasoning. She held herself back.

They sat at the long wood table. Anne took the head seat at the end. Ingrid scooted close to Adam. Anne placed her finds on the table. "These are great," Adam said. "How much do I owe you?"

"Oh, nothing, these are bar warming gifts. Ingrid told me about your plans."

"This is exactly what we're looking for. Can you find some larger items?" Adam held the whistle in his hand.

Anne pictured back to the sale where she'd seen the 1950s era red fire truck. She wondered if that was the larger item he was referring to. "Sure, give me an idea of what you're looking for and what you want to spend. We'll put you at the top of the list."

"Wait, a minute. Hey, Nick!" Adam got up, walked over to the firefighter stirring the chili. Nick turned around.

CC tipped her Ray-Bans down to drink in the tall, muscular firefighter. He looked 20 years Adam's senior. He had the face of a man who'd fought a lot of fires and won. His dark hair was peppered with a bit of gray. His face red and windburn. There was something about his eyes that held CC's. Not the color but the kindness that they exuded. CC felt a bit flustered.

"Hey Nick, these are my friends, Anne and CC. You met Ingrid already," Adam said. "Come sit down."

Nick looked around the table and sat at the bench seat next to CC. She could smell the smoke and Irish Spring on him. *Not unpleasant*, she thought.

"Nick's one of my partners in the bar. He's also the battalion leader."

Nick nodded his head at everyone and glanced at the antiques.

"Nick, Anne and CC are antique hunters. They've agreed to help us decorate the bar."

Nick nodded again. "Are you hungry?"

"It smells really good," CC said.

"Nick's going to do all the cooking at the bar. I'm going to bartend," Adam said.

Nick stood up and went back to stirring the chili. Anne pulled additional items from her bag to show Adam. CC went over to get a better look at the chili. "You cooked the kidney beans separately, right?"

"Yeah, otherwise they get too soft."

"I do the same thing. I like them a little crunchy. Do you mind if I taste it?"

Nick put a little on the ladle he was stirring with and placed it up to CC's lips. "Mmm, it's really good," she said.

"Not too hot? Not too spicy?" he asked.

"Not at all."

"I get some complaints from the guys that I make everything a little too spicy."

"Oh, no, it could never be too spicy for me. Are those chili and jalapeno peppers I taste?"

"Yeah, I grow them myself."

CC beamed and reached into her purse. She pulled out her small vial of ghost pepper powder. "This is from my garden. Have you ever had ghost peppers?"

He shook his head.

CC took the ladle from his hand, dipped it in the chili and sprinkled a little ghost pepper powder. She held her hand under the ladle and placed it toward his lips.

Nick tasted the peppers. CC was waiting for his response, waiting for the sweat to begin on his forehead and his face to flush. Instead he smiled. "That's the kick I was looking for. May I?"

CC handed him the tiny vial. He mixed it into the chili. She thought to herself, *it makes everything better.*

Chapter Twenty

Located in the northwest suburbs of Chicago, Ebbort Labs, one of the country's largest chemical testing facilities, used to be Anne's daytime home. She'd left to pursue her true calling—antique hunting. She had maintained her friendship with her former co-worker, Sharon.

She arrived at the lab after picking up Sharon's favorite Portillo's beef sandwich and met her at the back entrance. Sharon peeked around. "Are you sure you're good with this?" Anne asked.

Sharon handed her a visitor pass. "I talked to Dwayne out front. He said it's fine. We've both known you for years."

Anne clipped the visitor pass on her jacket, next to her art nouveau dragonfly brooch. The pass was not as spectacular but serviceable for the occasion. She followed Sharon to the laboratory where they'd worked together. "Great timing. Everyone else is at lunch. How's the antique hunting going?" Sharon asked.

"Great. I'm full time now."

"I wanted to go to your pop-up sale but couldn't make it. There was a baby shower for Deanna. You remember Deanna, don't you?" Sharon said, opening the paper bag.

"Sure." Anne nodded. She couldn't remember her at all. "Thanks so much for letting me do this." Anne plopped her belongings down in front of the microscope. Her cell phone rang. "Excuse me one minute," Anne said to Sharon before answering. "Hello," she said into the phone.

"Is this Anne Hillstrom?" the voice on the other end said.

"Yes, this is she."

"This is Sergeant Landis from the Chicago Police Department. Your car's in the impound lot on Pulaski if you want to pick it up," the voice on the other end said.

"You found it?" Anne exclaimed.

"We found it abandoned a mile from where you reported it missing."

"What about everything inside?" In Anne's mind, the contents were just as valuable—no, more valuable––than the car itself.

"It's still full of junk if that's what you mean."

"Junk?" Anne yelled back.

"Otherwise the car's in decent shape. It wasn't stripped. You can pick it up at the impound lot."

"Thank you." Anne hung up the phone and sat on the stool in front of the microscope. Sharon sat on the stool behind her, eating her cheesy beef and cheese fries.

"Help yourself," Sharon said.

Anne pulled the cake knife out of her bag. She took a small scraping from the back of handle, placing it in a chemical analyzer. The results were no surprise. Pure silver. Next was the emerald. Her hand shook a bit. She took a deep breath and calmed herself. She placed the knife under the refracting ultraviolet light. She dialed in the controls, flipping the switch. She closed her eyes for a second. When she opened them, she wanted to see the brilliant green of the emerald refracting its essence. She wanted to see the cake knife held by Marie Antoinette, days before the storming of the Bastille. Then the taking of Versailles before she lost her crown and her head. Anne whispered a prayer ending with, "Let them eat cake." She opened her eyes.

The stone refracted a brilliant red. She turned off the refracting ultraviolet light and sat down on the stool next to Sharon. She grabbed her cheesy beef croissant. She took a bite, mumbling, "Synthetic."

The lab doors swooshed open. A large man wearing a uniform, brandishing a Portillo's chili dog, burst into the room. "Anne, you gotta go. Everyone's getting back from lunch now. You gotta get out of here."

Anne hugged Sharon and grabbed her purse. As she was leaving, she tossed her visitor's pass at the security guard who called after her, "Thanks for the chili dogs but this was a one time deal. You can't come back. I could lose my job."

Chapter Twenty-one

CC rubbed the head of the world-famous Art Institute lion as she walked up the Chicago limestone steps. Ice and salt crunched under her Timberland boots. She stepped over to the other lion to rub his head. "You know, Ingrid, the south lion's unofficial name is *an attitude of defiance* while the north lion, here, his name is *on the prowl*. They were a gift from Mrs. Henry Field for the institute's opening in 1893. Of course, they were sculpted by the famous Edward Kemeys."

"You know so much, CC," Ingrid said.

CC smiled; it was a compliment of the highest order. They entered through the large doors. CC flashed her press pass, and the guide waved her and Ingrid in. "One stop before we go to the library," CC said. They entered the hall CC was looking for. Located on the second floor was the Art Institute's Impressionism exhibit. "There it is," CC said. On one entire wall hung Georges-Pierre Seurat's masterpiece *A Sunday Afternoon on the Island of La Grande Jatte*.

A line of elementary school kids all in uniform held hands staring at the painting as their teacher explained that it took Seurat two years to complete and that he created it with small brushstrokes, developing the technique called pointillism. As the children filed out, Ingrid and CC walked up, standing in front of the large painting.

"CC, that looks exactly like the desk," Ingrid said.

CC nodded as she marveled at the use of technique, light and color. "You know, Ingrid, Seurat was inspired by optical effects and perception. He contrasted the pigments with small brushstrokes so when they were unified optically, the human eye would perceive them as one shade."

After staring silently for a few more minutes, CC turned to Ingrid. "Let's go to the library," she said. They headed to the basement of the Art Institute. The Ryerson and Burnham Library was located in a small corner by the rotating exhibit hall. This month's exhibit featured photographs from young artists. They paused to study a few.

Inside the library, there were several wooden tables and comfortable chairs. The walls were lined with bookshelves. CC took it all in visually and then took a deep breath. "I love that smell, that library smell," she said.

"So what are we looking for?" Ingrid asked.

"I've checked online for any information about the Lycée Paris Art School. There's a lot about their famous students and teachers but what we're looking for is a list of all the students who attended the school. Specifically, after 1886 when Seurat first displayed his painting."

"How is that going to help us?"

"The initials J.C.T. on the desk. I couldn't find any famous painter with those initials but perhaps it will lead us to whoever scratched the drawing on the desk and help us value the desk."

"You think it could be worth a lot of money?"

"I think as it stands now it's worth a fair amount but if we can tie it in with the provenance of who sat at the desk and scratched the drawing, it could be worth more. More importantly, it's a mystery that needs to be solved," she said, smiling at Ingrid.

They each went towards separate bookshelves—CC to her favorite French impressionism, Ingrid to search through microfiches of Paris newspapers in the 1800s. By late afternoon, CC was exhausted. "Let's take a break for lunch," CC said to Ingrid.

They found the culinary student-run bistro. CC watched as the young chefs practiced their culinary arts. She observed a young girl, not much older than Ingrid, struggling as she attempted to butcher a chicken. The open kitchen called to CC, so she walked over. "Are you having a bit of trouble?"

The young girl glanced up, frustrated. Her instructor was nowhere to be seen. "We're making chicken de jonghe for dinner tonight. I have to butcher all the chickens and prepare the drumsticks."

"I can help with that." CC took the butcher knife, checked the edge and then took the honing rod, sharpening it. The young girl and Ingrid stood back, watching as CC dissected several chickens with the precision of a surgeon.

"Wow. Where'd you learn to do that?" the young girl asked.

"I grew up in Louisiana. Our neighbors had a chicken farm. At a pretty early age, I learned how to butcher chickens for Sunday dinner."

"You think you could help me prepare the chicken de jonghe?"

CC glanced over at the young girl's notebook. "Do you mind if I tweak the recipe a little bit?"

CC took a large cast iron skillet, put it on the stovetop. She turned the heat to moderate and toasted some coriander seeds. "You want to toast the seeds for about two minutes. When you can smell them, they're ready. Take them out and put them into a mortar. Wait until they're cool." Once the seeds had cooled, Ingrid ground them with a pestle.

In the same skillet, CC heated olive oil. "Let the olive oil get nice and hot. When it starts to shimmer, it's ready." She placed the drumsticks in the skillet, sprinkling salt and pepper on them. She turned them and waited until they turned a golden brown. She added onions, cooking them, stirring occasionally. "This should take about three minutes. You want the onions to be soft but not burnt," CC said. She added garlic, broth and the crushed coriander. She turned the heat down to low, covering the skillet. "Give yourself about fifteen minutes while you're preparing the sauce." In a small bowl, she whisked mustard with cream fraiche and tarragon. She removed the chicken, placing it on a platter. Then she whisked the mixture into the skillet. "You want to thicken the sauce for about four to five minutes." She returned the chicken to the skillet, spooning the sauce over it. She glanced around the kitchen, grabbing a loaf of French bread, cutting it up, smearing some Kerrygold butter on it. She plated three servings. The three sat at a corner table.

The young chef took a bite. "This is really good," she whispered. "Better than my teacher's."

"I'll write down the recipe for you. You prepare this tonight, and I think you'll get an *A*."

After they finished their meal and helped the young chef clean up, CC and Ingrid headed back to the library. The rest of the afternoon followed like the morning—not much to find. There were lots of articles and information about Degas, Renoir, Van Gogh. CC was about to call it a day when Ingrid called out, "CC, look." Ingrid waved at her.

CC returned the book she was reading to the shelf and went over to Ingrid. She glanced over her shoulder. "What is it?"

"I found this in a Paris newspaper. It's dated April 1882."

CC leaned in. The headline read, "Local Boy Drowns in Seine."

"What does it have to do with the desk?" CC asked.

"He was found floating off the isle of La Grande Jatte. His name is Jean Claude Tuffial—J.C.T.," Ingrid said. She read from the article, "The 13-year-old boy was the son of art supplier, Pierre Tuffial, resident of Montmartre. Where's Montmartre?"

"Interesting." CC sat back. "Montmartre was a rural village on the outskirts of Paris until it was annexed into the city. In the 1880s, Montmartre was home to many liberal students, artists and writers. Many popular artists like Degas and Renoir lived on its Grand Boulevard. There were also many art suppliers, vendors and galleries. Mr. Tuffial would have supplied the Paris art school with paints, easels and desks."

"You think his son, Jean Claude Tuffial, scratched his initials on the desk?"

"I think he would have gotten a beating from his dad if he did. The art suppliers of that day weren't wealthy. They were working class. And the boy died four years before Seurat showed his painting."

"Still, don't you think it's coincidental? The initials and that he drowned off the island? And that his father supplied the school?" Ingrid looked up from her seat at CC.

CC smiled at her apprentice. "Good catch, Ingrid."

Chapter Twenty-two

"I see you got your car back," CC said as Anne put on the teakettle. Ingrid moved the pile of newspapers on her kitchen table.

"Some stuff inside was tossed around but nothing seems to be missing," Anne said. "The car runs perfectly fine. It wasn't stripped or anything. Probably some kids took it for a joyride."

CC thought about the 25-year-old rust bucket. *Joyride, not likely.* "I'm glad they found it and it wasn't damaged. Where's Sassy?" CC asked.

"She's taken over the closet in the guest room. The vet said she'd probably prefer a quiet, out of the way place, so I cleared it out for her," Anne said.

"She's getting really close, isn't she?"

"Yes, I'm worried about her." The teakettle whistled. Anne poured each of them cups of tea in her Royal Doulton Bell Heather china. Its cheerful pink and green pattern reminded her of spring, a nice thought on this cold wintry day. She put out a tray of Italian wedding cookies that Grandma Jan had brought over earlier. She sat down next to them at the table.

"Anne, we're waiting. What did you find out about the cake knife?" CC asked.

Anne stirred three sugar cubes into her teacup and wiped powdered sugar off her blouse. She was too worried about Sassy to stay on her diet. She sipped her tea, placed the cup down and looked up. "The stone is synthetic. The cake knife is a replica. It's fake."

"Oh, I'm so sorry, Anne. I was hoping it was real," CC said. "Don't feel too down though. Ingrid and I have good news. At least I think it's good news. We found some information about the drawing desk. The initials *J.C.T.* we believe were scratched into the desk by Jean Claude Tuffial."

"Never heard of him," Anne said.

"He was the son of an art supply vendor in Montmartre."

"Oh, Montmartre," said Anne as she ran out of the room.

Ingrid and CC looked at each other, and then stood up in the archway, watching Anne flutter around the living room slaloming though the piles of books and bags and shiny things. She came to a screeching halt at her 1920 triple-door mahogany bookcase. She carefully inserted the skeleton key into the center door, ran her finger along several books, finally pulling out a large oversized coffee table book. Ingrid and CC ran back to the kitchen table and sat down. Anne came back into the kitchen, placed the leather-bound book triumphantly on the table. The image on the front showed the French countryside, its title in French: *Pictures of Montmartre.*

"I had forgotten about this book. It has some really beautiful illustrations. I found it at an estate sale for an art gallery in the Left bank. I thought at one point I was going to cut some of the illustrations out and frame them. I changed my mind and decided I wanted to leave the book in its original state. It's from the late 1800s. It's all in French so I couldn't make hide nor hair of it."

CC carefully turned the book around so it was facing her, opening it. "This is very beautiful, Anne. The illustrations are amazing."

"Yes."

CC read the copyright page. "It says each illustration was drawn by a local artist. I think this is almost like a portfolio of young artists in the area. I don't recognize any of the names of the artists." She stopped at a page. It was a drawing of a sailboat on the Seine River. The background behind the sailboat was the island of La Grande Jatte. CC read its caption: "Jean Claude Tuffial."

"That's the name! That's the artist you were talking about," Anne said.

"Yes, the copyright date is 1881. This is a year before he drowned." All three Spoon Sisters crowded over the top of the book, admiring the illustration.

"It's really very good. The detail."

CC noticed something in the background. She pulled out her jeweler's loupe. "Ingrid, take a look." She handed the loupe to Ingrid.

"What is it?" Anne asked, unable to control herself.

After looking at the image, Ingrid handed the loupe to Anne. "It's a monkey."

"Yes," CC said. "Like the monkey in Seurat's painting."

Before they could ponder any more on it, they heard a bloodcurdling screech. "Sassy!" Anne leapt up. She ran up the stairs to the second floor bedroom, Ingrid and CC on her heels, skipping over the piles of books, baskets and clothes.

Anne screeched to a halt in the hallway. By the dim light of the vintage enamel hurricane lamp, she watched as her beloved Sassy birthed three perfectly white Persian kittens.

Chapter Twenty-three

"Dear Friends, exciting news!" CC typed on her laptop. "Sassy is now a mother. Three beautiful white Persians yet to be named. Mother and kittens are doing well. Anne is excited and already out shopping for kitten toys and beds. They are a day old but she wants to be ready."

CC stopped for a moment, sipped her coffee and then continued typing, "I want to thank you again for the wonderful turnout at our previous pop-up sale. I apologize about canceling the second sale. Anne continues to sort through items and will contact those of you on our lists whose requests we can fill. More to come later." She posted the blog.

She opened her Google search engine and went to ancestry.com. She typed in Jean-Claude Tuffial. A long list of records with the last name appeared on the search screen. She checked Paris 1882 and found a death certificate for Jean-Claude. Cause of death was listed as drowning. His parents were named as Pierre and Margarite. A newspaper article similar to the one Ingrid had found confirmed that his father was a local art supply merchant in Montmartre and that he had a brother Jacques. She followed Jacques' branch to his son Michael, born 1901 in Baltimore, Maryland. Michael's son, George, was born in 1925, still in Maryland. George's daughter, Jacqueline, born 1945, in Biloxi, Mississippi. Father died in World War II. Jacqueline married Tim Guido in 1968 in Louisville, Kentucky. Daughter Jacqueline Guido born in 1970 in

Indianapolis. She Googled Jacqueline Guido, Indianapolis. A website came up. Jacqueline was a well-known Midwest landscape painter with a gallery/studio in downtown Indianapolis.

CC called the studio. A young woman answered, "Guido Studios."

"I'd like to speak to Jacqueline Guido."

"Who may I say is calling?"

"My name is CC Muller. I'm a reporter from Chicago."

"Let me see if she's available." The woman placed the phone on hold and left.

A few minutes later, another woman answered, "This is Jacqueline. How may I help you?"

"I'm CC Muller. I'm a journalist in Chicago. I'm researching a story about neo-impressionism."

"That's not my specialty."

"Actually the story has to do with the Montmartre movement in the late 1800s."

Jacqueline didn't say anything.

"I'd like to ask you some questions about Jean-Claude Tuffial."

"How do you know that name?"

"I stumbled across it at the Art Institute. My colleague and I travel to estate sales and we recently purchased some items at the sale of an art school in Paris. One of the items was a desk with the initials J.C.T. on it. I wondered if that could be your relative."

"I have some time this afternoon if you want to come out to the studio."

CC jotted down the address. As CC hung up the phone, she saw Ingrid enter the kitchen wearing nothing but a Glen Ellyn Fire Department t-shirt. She was smoothing her ruffled hair. CC jumped up, running up the stairs. She flung open Ingrid's bedroom door. She let out a sigh when she saw it was empty. She went back downstairs and found Ingrid stirring batter in her splatter ware bowl. "What time did you get in last night? I fell asleep. I didn't hear you."

Ingrid turned around with a smile. "Adam and I went to the midnight movie of *Rocky Horror*."

"Oh, Adam?" CC stared pointedly at the shirt.

"I spilled my coke on my top while we were watching the movie. People were throwing toast and toilet paper at the screen. It surprised me. Adam had an extra t-shirt in his truck."

"Oh, then."

"What's wrong, cousin CC?"

"I worry about you. You're in a strange country, strange men."

"Men are the same in every country," Ingrid interrupted.

"Yes, but you're a beautiful young girl and it's my responsibility to keep you safe."

"Safe from what?"

"Well, you know."

"No, I don't know," Ingrid said with a half smirk.

"Don't make me get into this conversation. I promised your mother I'd watch out for you."

Ingrid went over and sat at the chair next to CC. She put her hand on her knee. "Cousin CC, I appreciate it. I'm eighteen; I can take care of myself."

"Do me a favor. Take this." CC ran out of the room and came back in a few minutes carrying a tiny vial of ground ghost pepper. "This is from my summer garden. It's ghost pepper. It's a hundred times hotter than jalapeno or any pepper spray you can buy on the market. Keep it in your purse. If the need arises, this will do the trick. Throw it in an attacker's face; it will blind him, giving you time to run away. It makes everything better."

"Danke." Ingrid went back to the counter and beat the batter.

"What are you making?"

"My mom's German pancakes." Ingrid melted butter in a cast iron pan. She stirred together flour, milk and eggs and poured it into the pan. She then put it into the oven. Ingrid set the timer on the stove. "I'm going to take a shower while this is baking."

"I'm going to get ready, too." CC stood up. "We're heading to Indianapolis to see Jean-Claude Tuffial's great-great-grand niece."

Chapter Twenty-four

After picking up Anne, CC drove the VW bus on I-294 south towards Indianapolis. "I found an amazing antique store in Indianapolis. It's called Midland Antiques. It's in an old factory downtown. We have to stop," Anne said. "CC, you'll love it. According to the *Yelp* reviews, it has a lot of primitives and industrial antiques."

"We should have time to stop. We're not meeting Jacqueline until 2 p.m.," CC said.

The gravel parking lot of the warehouse crackled under the VW bus tires. The red brick warehouse filled an entire block. Hung above the metal door, facing the parking lot was a crudely hand drawn sign that read *Antiques.* Anne went up the uneven steps followed by an enthusiastic Ingrid. CC stopped to examine the garden statues scattered around, thinking about her backyard.

Anne wandered haphazardly from booth to booth, picking up items and then setting them back down, remembering she was broke. She pulled the notebook with their fan list requests from her bag, scanning it. This old wooden top would be perfect for Charles from Colorado. A few aisles over, she spotted a pair of mother-of-pearl opera glasses just like Amanda from Los Angeles was looking for. A large four-foot Lucas oil bright ceramic sign produced another check on her list—a match for Jeremy from Ohio working on his man cave garage. By the time she was done, she had a pull cart full of fan request antiques and maybe she had snuck in one or two things for herself including an early edition leather-bound copy of *War and Peace*.

CC snuck up behind her, startling her. "Anne, what's all this?"

Anne held up her notebook. "Fan list. These are all requests for the fan list."

"How are you going to pay for them?"

Anne shrugged. She was spared having to answer when Ingrid came up to her. "Anne, can you come here? I want your opinion on something."

She followed Ingrid over to a booth which was filled with tools and primitive materials. Ingrid pointed to a cast iron horse-drawn fire wagon, which took up more than half the booth. Anne studied its construction. "This is a great find, Ingrid. It must be from the late 1800s."

"What do you think? For Adam?" Ingrid asked.

"That would look great in the front of the bar," Anne agreed. The tag said $1,800. "I think we could negotiate with them." She paused. "Let's think about it while we walk around."

CC walked over to an early oil painting of a silo. Anne took out her iPhone and dialed her bank. She checked her bank balance through the automated system and plopped down in the middle of the floor. "$112,000." She hit *zero* for customer service. The perky voice on the other end informed her that all her funds had been restored as the bank had determined the recent withdrawals had been fraud.

Life returned to Anne. She could breath again. She left her overflowing cart by the register and grabbed an empty one. By the time CC went up to the register, Anne had seven carts full. "Really, Anne?"

"CC, good news. The bank refunded all my money," Anne exclaimed. "I'm rich again."

"That's great but you can't buy all this," CC said. "What about your bills? The mortgage?"

Anne ran up and down the seven carts, attempting to add the price tags in her head. She pushed one cart out of line. CC crossed her arms and gave her a look. Anne timidly pushed one more cart out of line.

"Anne, I can't fit all this in the VW."

"We'll come back."

"Pick one cart. Every item must be on the list and then whatever profit you make from that goes into your savings." As CC spoke, Anne pushed the largest cart to the register. CC smiled and walked away.

"I have a plique du jour diamond and gold grasshopper brooch that you're holding," Anne whispered to the clerk. "Add that and wrap it quickly. I'll put it in my bag. We'll also take the antique fire hose wagon. Someone will pick it up later."

The girl behind the counter handed Anne the wrapped brooch. She shoved it into her bag and paid for the rest of her purchases. "That was fun, Anne," Ingrid said, admiring her 1970s leather fringe jacket. "Thanks for buying me the jacket." She swirled around, watching the fringe of the vintage leather jacket chase behind her.

CC came out behind them, carrying one small bag and a glass bottle. She glanced at Ingrid wearing the jacket, but didn't have the energy to ask about it. They loaded the VW and headed to downtown Indianapolis, just a seven-minute drive.

Anne's eyes lit up when she saw the picturesque square. It was dotted with cute shops, an overhead-enclosed walkway leading to fabulous shopping. A human habitrail for shopping enthusiasts. She watched as the hamsters strolled through the walkway, arms laden with shopping bags. And she couldn't help but notice the clock tower.

As they drove by, CC swerved for a second as she glanced at the former railroad station. The station was an icon for the city with its huge clock tower, circular mosaic window, slate roof and corner bartizans. "You know, Anne, that building was America's first union station. This is where most of Indiana's first immigrants landed. It was built by architect Thomas Rodd in the Romanesque Revival style," CC said. "There it is," she added, stopping in front of a small storefront. "Get out of the car. I'll look for parking." Anne and Ingrid got out and entered the storefront.

CC circled the block and finally found meter parking in front of the store. She could see Anne through the window, talking to a young woman about a painting on the wall, her hands flailing around, reaching into her large orange Prada bag for her checkbook.

CC ran inside. "Anne."

Anne froze.

CC went up to them. "We're here to see Jacqueline Guido. We have an appointment."

"Ms. Muller, follow me. She's expecting you." They followed the young woman to the back room. Easels with paintings lined the room. Floor to ceiling plate glass windows covered the entire west side of the building. The early afternoon sunlight chased shadows away. A wooden desk stood in the middle of the room. It was the art studio that CC had dreamed of.

"Thanks for agreeing to meet us," CC said.

Jacqueline rose to shake CC's hand. She was wearing jeans and a paint-covered t-shirt. Her long salt and pepper hair was pulled back in a ponytail. Crystal stone jewelry dangled from her wrists and neck.

"These are my friends, Anne and Ingrid," CC said.

"Of course, the Spoon Sisters. I Googled you after we spoke. Please, let's go sit." They walked to a couch and some chairs grouped in a corner of the large space. Jacqueline sat down and lit a cigarette. "You don't mind, do you?"

They all shook their heads. "I told you about the Art Institute and the article. Is Jean-Claude Tuffial related to you?" CC asked.

"Yes, he was my great-grandfather's brother. You said you were doing a story about the neo-impressionist movement. From what I understand, he was just a kid—talented—but still not important enough to write about."

CC sat next to Jacqueline, pulling out her iPad mini and bringing up a photo of the desk. The second photo shot ten feet away revealed the carving. Jacqueline recognized it right away. "That carving has the initials J.C.T.," CC said. She pulled up another picture from Anne's Montmartre book. Jacqueline recognized it immediately. "Yes, I know that drawing. You can see the potential. That's Jean-Claude's."

Jacqueline stood up, walked across the room to a steel utility cabinet. She came back, carrying a large leather portfolio. "After you called, I hunted for these." She placed the folio on the coffee table, opening it to reveal black and white sketches. "All these are what my great-great-grandfather had left from his brother. He died when he was thirteen." They were drawings of Montmartre, the island of La Grande Jatte, Paris cityscapes and a self-portrait.

"This is him?" Anne held up a drawing from the portfolio of a young boy.

"Yes." Jacqueline nodded.

The drawing was not as precise as the other ones. It was almost more like a surrealistic work. "This one is so different than the rest."

"Yes, that's Jean-Claude probably months before he drowned. When he turned 13, he began having seizures. It got so bad from what I understand that his right hand shook constantly. He started drawing with his left. Eventually, from what my grandfather told me, he would have to tie his arm down to the easel to keep it steady enough to paint. That's why it looks so scribbled. He couldn't lift his hand more than an inch away from the canvas without it shaking uncontrollably. The seizures got worse. That's how they believe he drowned. They think he had a grand mal seizure off the island while he was swimming."

"That's horrible," Anne said.

"Did he visit the island often?" CC asked.

"He would go there on the weekends and paint portraits for pennies. He had saved enough money to attend one semester at the Lycée Paris art school. That was the year he drowned."

As Jacqueline spoke, CC found a sketch of the island. Women with parasols, a monkey at their feet. What caught her eye most was the profile of a man, very faint but distinguishable, because she was looking for it. She showed it to Anne and then to Jacqueline. "This is Seurat."

Jacqueline took a closer look, holding it up to the afternoon sun. She said, "I never noticed that before but I'm not surprised. It was the same time period and Jean-Claude would have sold supplies to Degas, Renoir and Seurat." She paused. "Are you telling me that Jean-Claude sat at the desk you found?"

"I believe so," CC said.

Chapter Twenty-five

"Perfect." Anne said. Ingrid nodded in agreement as they admired the antique fire wagon in its new location outside the bar.

"We're still waiting on the sign. That's supposed to be here this week," Adam said, opening the oak fortress door. Anne, Ingrid and CC stood in the open bar; boxes and crates lined the wood plank floors. A huge rosewood bar covered the entire length of one wall. Its front was adorned with elaborate scrollwork and a large brass foot rail. Behind it, hung a large beveled mirror. "Nick found that at a demolition sale."

"Did I hear my name?" Nick came out of the back room, wiping his hands on a towel. His navy blue Glen Ellyn Fire Department t-shirt strained across his broad chest.

CC smiled. He returned her smile.

"Hey, Nick, I was telling the girls about how you found the bar," Adam said, draping his arm around Ingrid.

"Yeah, it was at an old Irish pub in the city that was being torn down for condos. Progress," Nick said sarcastically.

"What a shame. I'm glad you were able to rescue it," CC said, running her hands along the carved edge of the bar.

"When will you be ready to open?" Anne asked.

"Hopefully, within the month. We're going to do a soft launch with social media and then a larger grand opening," Adam said, stepping behind the bar.

"First we have to get our permit and liquor license approved by the village board," Nick added, leaning against the bar.

"We're trying to get organized," Adam said, opening a box of bar glasses. One by one, Ingrid took the glasses out of the box and placed them onto the wood shelves.

"I need to get back. I'm working on the kitchen," Nick said, heading toward the back room.

"Can I help?" CC asked.

"I'd appreciate it." He smiled at her.

CC followed him into the back room, a galley gleaming with brand new stainless steel appliances and countertops. "You know, I wrote a story about the popularity of stainless steel in kitchens. Its use started with industrial applications and spread because of sanitary reasons," she said.

"Is that right?" Nick asked, hanging pots on hooks above the counter. His biceps bulged as he reached overhead.

CC felt the heat of the kitchen. Not the gas stove but the man standing by it. She hadn't been close to a man in a while. "What would you like me to do?" she asked. For a moment, her question hung in mid-air.

"You can unpack the silverware." Nick pointed at several boxes by the back door.

"Sure, be glad to," she said, opening a box and putting the silverware in the sink to wash them.

"Wait," Nick said. He ran over to one of the crisp white aprons hanging in the corner. He ran back and draped it over CC's head. He reached around her side and tied it firmly around her waist, his chest rubbing against her back. As Nick's hands lingered, Anne peeked into the kitchen. Before she could say anything, she saw Nick's hands around her friend. She tiptoed quietly back out. Nick's hands lingered for a moment longer. Then he went back to hanging pots and CC returned to breathing. CC piled the flatware into the sink.

Adam stepped into the room. "Hey Nick, we're going to grab a pizza. Do you want to come with us?"

Nick glanced at CC who shook her head. "I'm going to finish unpacking here," he said.

"I'll stay and help if you don't mind," CC said, looking at Nick.

"See you guys, later." Adam left the kitchen. Nick and CC could hear the front door close.

When CC finished cleaning the silverware, she helped unpack the pots and pans. They arranged the utensils near the stove. When they were done, CC wiped her hands on her apron. Nick was cooking something in a frying pan. CC walked over and sniffed. "That smells great," she said, peering around his shoulder.

"It's fresh cod I picked up today. Not something that will be on the menu." Nick added some garlic, a half-cup of melted butter, lemon juice and salt and pepper to the fish. While that was simmering, he chopped a head of cauliflower, sautéed it in olive oil and then mixed in breadcrumbs and Parmesan and put it in the oven. "Would you like some wine?"

"Oh, I almost forgot." She ran out of the kitchen, came back shortly with a bottle of wine. "Unfortunately it's red and you're making fish. It's from my garden. It's cherry wine."

Nick walked over to a cabinet and brought out a bottle without a label. "I made this from white grapes I grow in my backyard." He opened the bottle and poured a glass.

CC sniffed, swirled and sipped. She smiled. *It might even be better than hers*, she thought, *but she was okay with that.* "It's a very good vintage." She flipped her hair over her shoulder—this time not even meaning to do it. It was more of a subconscious reaction to the wine, the fish and the fireman. She thought to herself, *that* would be a good title for a book. She giggled and polished off her glass.

Nick plated the fish and the cauliflower. They sat on the high stainless steel stools. CC took a bite. The fish was flaky, buttery and sweet. "This fish is perfect, Nick. The guys at the firehouse must love your cooking."

"It's a little more basic there. It's nice to have a chance to experiment."

CC watched as Nick cut his fish. She noticed the burn mark on his arm for the first time. Nick caught her looking and raised his arm up. "It was five years ago. I ran into a house and a burning rafter landed on me. It pinned me for a couple minutes. It seemed longer, burning me right through my gear."

"How'd you make it out?"

"My guys carried me out. The whole floor was a wall of fire."

CC took another bite. She didn't know how to respond. "Why the bar?"

"We're two days on, one day off. The firehouse becomes your home, more of a home than your house. When you walk out of there after 48 hours on, it seems kind of strange to go home especially if you live alone. The bar is a second home. I wanted a place where the guys could come after a couple tough days and relax."

"I get it." CC nodded. "The place looks great. I'm glad we could help out with the decor. I understand what you mean about a bar. There's something familiar, comforting. It's cool and dark and there's no sense of time. I like that."

Nick filled her wine glass. CC was on her third glass. When they were done cleaning the kitchen, she glanced around at the shiny surfaces. She stood awkwardly, running her fingers along the stainless countertop. "I should get going."

"I'll walk you out." He led the way out the front door and followed CC to the VW. CC stopped by the driver's door. Nick reached around, opened it for her.

"Thank you," she said. She sat in the driver's seat for a moment, took a breath, started the VW up. She gave Nick a glance before driving away. She promised herself she wouldn't look in the rearview mirror. If Nick was still standing in front of the bar, she would regret leaving and if he wasn't standing watching her drive away, then she would regret not kissing him goodbye. She kept her eyes on the road ahead of her.

Chapter Twenty-six

CC carefully wiped the drawing desk top with a solution of Murphy's soap and water, rubbing the cheesecloth softly around the top. Once it was dry, she draped the four-foot sheet of rice paper over the top, using masking tape to hold down the edges. Anne and Ingrid watched fascinated. Sassy lay on Anne's living room floor, cleaning her three kittens. CC took the rubbing crayon and began rubbing the paper against the desk, bringing the drawing to life. She had learned this technique when she was researching genealogy and making gravestone etchings.

When she'd finished, they headed to CC's house and down to her basement. She hung the rice paper on a large canvas balanced on an easel. Using her medium format black and white Hasselblad 500CM, she took a picture of the etching. She stepped into her darkroom and developed the shots. With her enlarger, she compressed the negative so that all the tiny dots on the desktop combined the puzzle to give her a clear picture. When she left the darkroom, Anne was sitting on the couch next to Ingrid, educating her on shopping on eBay.

"You know we have eBay in Germany, too," Ingrid said.

"What it's called there?"

"eBay. Here's some of the items I'm watching." Ingrid and Anne peered onto Ingrid's smartphone screen.

CC cleared her throat. Anne stuck her phone between the seat cushions. CC placed the photograph on her light table. Anne and Ingrid peered over her shoulder. "Wow. That looks exactly like Seurat's painting two years before he painted it," Anne said.

"It is, but it's from a reverse angle." CC placed an 8 x 10 picture of Seurat's drawing next to it. "In the background, you can see Seurat staring at Jean-Claude. It's two different viewpoints of the same subject."

"Jacqueline said that Jean-Claude spent his weekends on the island. Seurat must have seen him painting portraits and landscapes with his shaking hand. His paintings becoming thousands of dots. He gave Seurat the idea."

"My desk," Anne said. "It has to be worth a fortune."

"We have to bring it to the Art Institute."

"We're not going to donate it, are we?" Anne asked.

"This could change art history. It's like saying the Mona Lisa wasn't painted by Da Vinci or that David wasn't created by Michelangelo." CC paused. "We have to get in touch with the professor." She picked up her phone and dialed his number. "It's been disconnected," she said to Anne.

"Why don't you call the Art Institute? Maybe they know how to get in touch with him," Anne said.

CC dialed the Art Institute. She spoke into the phone and then hung up. "They never heard of him. There's no Professor Gildwin who works there or is associated with the Art Institute."

"Are you sure?"

"Yeah, they checked."

Anne dialed Nigel. "Hey, Nigel, it's Anne. Do you have a minute?"

"Yes, of course, Anne. I was actually going to call you. We recovered some of the stolen items from your purse. Well, actually *we* didn't. The Wheaton police department recovered a silver monogrammed pillbox with your name and address inside."

"What do you mean?"

"After you told me about the man who took your purse, I contacted the Wheaton police and told them to call me if they found out anything. They caught the man. He was trying to pawn a bunch of items that were stolen from the flea market. He has a record of aggravated assault and burglary, a pretty bad bloke."

"Oh. So, he wasn't after me?"

"Why would he be after you? Are you in trouble?"

"No, Nigel, it's just since the poor sweet shop lady, I haven't felt safe."

"There's no evidence that the man who killed the sweet shop lady was at your store for you. It's still under investigation." Nigel paused. "And, the purse snatching at the flea market was a coincidence. There were several purse snatchings that night." Nigel paused again. "Is that why you called me?"

"No, actually, I—I mean *we*, CC and I—need your help. We need you to track down an address for us. I have a name and cell phone number."

"What's this for?"

"He's one of our clients."

"Why don't you call him?"

"It's a long story. Can you trust me on this?"

"You know I care for you and I want to help you. That's the problem. I always want to help you."

"I'm not asking you on a date. I need your professional help."

Nigel hesitated, the dead air on the phone was stagnant. "You're asking me to step over the line again, Anne."

"Nigel," Anne said in her softest, sweetest voice. "I know I ask a lot of you, and I don't give a lot back. I know it's not fair, but I do care about you. Your friendship is very important to me. The man we want to track down, Professor Gildwin, is trying to buy an antique from us. An antique we just learned may be very valuable. He's lied to us about who he is. My containers were tampered with. The sweet shop lady was killed and somehow I think it all leads back to the professor."

"Anne, you and CC come into the office. You need to report everything you know."

"Nigel, that's all we know. We can't prove anything."

"Anne this is the last time. Give me his name and number. I'll text you his address." With that, the very tall and very British detective Nigel Towers ended the conversation and any hope of romance.

Chapter Twenty-seven

CC rang the buzzer outside the professor's aluminum-sided one-story house in Chicago's near north Rogers Park area. "You sure this is the right address?" CC asked, as they stared at the dilapidated building.

Anne checked her text message again. "Yep, this is it."

"It's not the kind of building I imagine an art professor living in," Ingrid said.

CC cupped her hands around her face, trying to peek through the storm window door. Anne pulled her parka tight around her neck. The sun was dropping, so was the temperature. CC rang the doorbell again.

The curtains moved. CC knocked on the door. "Professor, we know you're in there. We want to talk to you," she said.

They heard a click and the door swung open. Professor Gildwin stood in front of them, in his flannel bathrobe and slippers. "What are you doing here? How did you get my address?"

"We need to talk to you about the desk," CC said.

"You're here now. Come in." He held the door open. They entered the living room, which was crowded with bookcases and books on top of books. He cleared some newspapers off the couch and motioned for them to sit down. Anne wandered around the bookcases, examining the titles. He brought up a small wooden chair, sitting across from CC.

"We know that you don't work with the Art Institute," CC said.

The professor reached in his robe pocket, pulled out a pack of cigarettes. He held it up, offering it to CC. She shook her head. "Do you mind if I smoke?" Before they could answer, he lit his cigarette and inhaled. "It's been ten years since I worked there. Artistic differences, you might say," he said with a smirk as he took another puff.

"Why is the desk so important to you?" CC asked. Anne pulled a book on neo-impressionism off the shelf and breezed through its pages. She appreciated his book selection.

The professor got up and took a thick binder full of typewritten pages off one of the bookshelves. He put it on the small, shaky coffee table. "1,298 pages; that's my life's work."

CC opened the binder, scribbled on the first page was *Seurat*. "When I did work, I taught a satellite class at the Art Institute on neo-impressionists. I gave lectures on Seurat and pointillism. I can't tell you how many hours, days, months, I spent staring at that painting. One thing always bothered me. Something that stuck in my head, kept me up at night." He flipped through the pages of his manuscript. "Seurat said some may see poetry in my paintings but I see only science. He was fascinated by the color theories of scientists like Ogden Rood. He explored divisionism."

CC interrupted. "Divisionism is the method that uses color in patches. It tricks the human eye into blending them, creating luminescence and shape."

"Exactly." The professor nodded. "All the figures in the painting are looking away at the water, at the park, except for one."

"The little girl in white," CC said.

"She's staring directly at Seurat. There are many theories of who the little girl is, was and why he painted her staring at him. Some say it was to show the innocence of a lovely afternoon. Some say its Seurat's own insecurities as a young artist. That the little girl is the only one who knows that Seurat is a fraud. Seurat often struggled with his art."

"How did that lead you to the desk and Jean-Claude Tuffial?"

He flipped through the pages in his binder, revealing an illustration torn from a sketchbook. "I found this in the Art Institute archives. Well, I stole it from the archives."

CC examined the illustration. It was a crude drawing of the little girl from Seurat's *Sunday in the Park*. The initials were J.C.T.

"I became obsessed by this portrait of Seurat's little girl sketched by another artist. I spent years researching, trying to prove my theory."

"What theory?"

"That Seurat didn't paint *Sunday Afternoon*. That it was this artist, J.C.T. You can imagine the Art Institute's reaction to my theory that their most famous painting was a fraud. I was ostracized by the art world. The Art Institute let me go. My lectures were an embarrassment to the Institute. I never stopped my research. When I saw the photos you posted on your blog of the desk and I could see the scratches on the desk which created the faint image of a drawing, I wasn't sure. But when you posted the initials J.C.T., I was."

Anne couldn't hold back any longer. "It was you," she said. "You broke into my containers, my garage. It was you who killed the sweet shop lady."

"I don't know what you're talking about," the professor said. "I was promised that desk. I'm the one

who told you about the art school sale. I'm not a killer."
The professor's hand shook as he lit another cigarette.

"We'll let the police figure that out," Anne said. She
reached into her pocket, pulling out her iPhone.

The professor rose to his feet, knocking the phone
onto the floor. "This is my life's work!" His eyes were
wild. He reached into his robe pocket.

Quicker to the draw, Anne reached inside her large
orange Prada bag. In one motion, she retrieved the cake
knife and served up justice on the professor's head,
knocking him out cold. "Let them eat cake," Anne said,
standing triumphantly over him.

As the police arrived and handcuffed the professor,
CC reached into the professor's robe pocket to see what
he was reaching for. It was a postcard of *Sunday in the
Park*. She had the same one on her refrigerator. CC
looked at the card, then at the professor. "Seurat did
paint *Sunday in the Park*. The little girl in the portrait is
a tribute to Jean-Claude Tuffial, who Seurat watched
paint portraits on Sundays on the island of La Grande
Jatte. The boy had epilepsy. His hand shook so badly
that his last paintings were scribbled into dots from his
hand lifting on and off the canvas. That's what gave
Seurat the idea of pointillism."

The professor opened his mouth, only silence came
out.

Chapter Twenty-eight

Anne made tea while Ingrid and CC watched. Ingrid held one of Sassy's kittens, stroking her soft white fur. "CC, can we keep one?"

"Ingrid, let me educate you on the Australian shepherd breed. They are all alphas. They herd and corral everything, even people. Our house would not be a good environment for a kitten."

Ingrid rubbed her cheek against the tiny kitten as it purred. Sassy watched from her perch above the kitchen table. The other two kittens played on the floor. Anne filled the teacups, handing them out, sitting down at the table. "I've already decided Grandma Jan is going to take one."

"How does she feel about that?" CC asked.

"I'm not sure yet but I don't want Snowball going too far from Sassy."

"Snowball?"

"That's what I'm calling her. Temporarily. She's the fat one." Anne sipped her tea followed by a bite of the sugar cookie. "And that one Snowball is playing with is promised to Nigel for helping us out."

"When did that happen?"

"After the professor was arraigned, Nigel and I talked in the courthouse hallway. He's not seeing Betsy anymore. That kitten I'm calling Poppy, short for Mary Poppins. Nigel and I love that movie."

CC looked over to the last little kitten who was sound asleep in Ingrid's arms. "That little angel, I'm keeping. I've not thought of a name for her yet. She has a curious personality. Out of all the kittens, she gets into the most trouble. She hides in my hatboxes and steals my earrings. She's fascinated by my antiques."

Snowball climbed up on the counter, knocking over the cake knife. It hit the floor. "Snowball!" Anne scolded the kitten, chocolate frosting all over her whiskers. Anne picked up the knife. "Oh, look, the stone popped out. Help me find it." Before Anne could search the floor, Poppy triumphantly carried the stone out from underneath the table. Anne reached down. "I guess I can glue it back in." She sat down at the table, trying to fit the stone back in place. "That's funny." She shook the handle. It rattled. She flipped the knife over with the handle upside down and tapped on the back. Out popped a deep blue heart-shaped stone. "Why would there be another stone behind the green one? This one is really imitation. Look, it's heart shaped. That's hokey. I hate heart-shaped jewelry and I hate the color blue. My cake knife is ruined." She absentmindedly ran the blue stone along the top of the table. "Oh, dear, stupid stone scratched my table protector."

CC touched the protector. "Anne, what is this made of?"

"I bought it to protect the wood underneath. Between Sassy and everyday wear, the wood was getting pretty scratched up. This table is over a hundred years old."

"What's it made of?"

"Well, glass. I went to Ace and had them cut the exact dimensions. That way I could see the wood underneath it."

CC took the heart-shaped stone and rubbed it across the table, leaving behind a trail of scratches. "What are you doing? You're ruining the glass," Anne said.

"A synthetic stone wouldn't scratch the glass like this. You know that!" CC pulled her loupe out and held the stone, shining her pen flashlight behind it. "Anne, this is real! This is beautiful. This has to be a five carat blue diamond. You know what that's worth?"

"Don't start again. I went through this with the synthetic emerald. They can make them look real."

"No, Anne, I'm telling you, a synthetic stone would not scratch the glass like that. I really think this is real. Why else would they have hidden it inside the handle? Why hide a synthetic stone behind a synthetic stone?" CC said. "Gregg Ludicki told me that the man who died on the plane, Bernie, was an import/exporter. What if he was dealing in stolen jewels?"

CC blew on the stone. The fog from her breath disappeared instantly. "What are you doing, CC?" Anne asked.

"Real diamonds propagate heat. When you blow on it, if it fogs up and doesn't clear right away, it's a fake. This one is obviously real."

Anne shook her head, still not believing. CC took a newspaper off the pile. She placed the stone on top of it. She stared down into it. "I can't see anything."

Anne looked at Ingrid. "A fake diamond won't refract the light like a genuine diamond. You'd be able to read the newspaper through it. A real diamond refracts light so sharply you can't see the print through it." Anne grabbed the stone from CC. "I'm still not convinced. I need to find if it *is* real. If it *is* real, I need to find out what's it worth. I can't go back to the lab."

"Why don't you call Amy and make an appointment to have her appraise the stone?" CC asked.

"Who's Amy?" Ingrid asked.

"An old friend," Anne said. "She buys and sells diamonds for Tiffany's, Cartier and Neiman Marcus. She has a jewelry store downtown on Wabash Avenue."

"You know, Ingrid, Wabash is known as Jeweler's Row because historically it's been home to many wholesale jewelers." CC turned back to Anne, "Amy will know if it's real or not. You and Ingrid follow the diamond. I'm going to talk to Gregg to see if I can find out more about Bernie," CC said.

Chapter Twenty-nine

"Dear Friends," CC wrote on the blog. "So much catching up to do. So many things have happened since the pop-up sale. I've attached a picture of the drawing desk that Anne bought in Paris. What you didn't know is the mystery behind it. Picture Two shows the underside of the top of the desk. You can see it's a mirror image of Seurat's *Sunday in the Park on La Grand Jatte*. After doing some investigating, we discovered that a young Phenom artist in Montmartre named Jean-Claude Tuffial made this scratching before Seurat even had the idea of painting *Sunday Afternoon*. The two had met several times on the island. The young boy who was afflicted with epilepsy learned to paint with a shaky hand in what scholars now call pointillism. Quite a story. Even more intriguing is Professor Gildwin who had tasked us with finding antiques from the closing of the art school. He turned out not to be who he said he was. The matter is under police investigation for now but we will update you as we learn more. The good news is that the desk has found its home at the Art Institute. Here is a picture of Anne signing it over to the curator. Ignore the look on her face. She eventually gave into the idea that it was the best place for the desk to be. A small plaque will be placed next to the desk acknowledging Anne's contribution.

"We've had so many requests for another pop-up sale that I'm pleased to announce next Saturday we'll have our final close-out spectacular. It's been so much fun meeting all of you in person. We had to have one more hurrah. I've listed all the items, most of them coming directly from Anne's personal collection. See you there. Au revoir."

CC closed her laptop, ruffled the fur on Bandit's head who was lying on the floor under her desk. She finished her last drop of French press coffee, thinking about the cup she drank on the Champs-Elysees and about the cute waiter who flirted with her. At least she thought he was flirting. Then her mind turned to the task at hand, calling Gregg. "Hello, Gregg, it's CC," she said.

"CC, I'm so glad you called."

"Yes, nice to speak with you. I was wondering if you could answer some questions about Bernie Gladstone."

"What kind of questions? I thought we went through all this." Gregg's tone changed to irritation.

"Just to tie up some loose ends, to clear things up."

"Is this about a story?"

"No, just my own curiosity."

Gregg was silent for a moment, "Why don't we meet for drinks?"

CC put her iPhone down, took a deep breath. The last thing she wanted to do was meet Gregg for drinks. "Really, all I want to know is a little bit about his history. Do you know where's he traveled in the last year or so?"

"I don't have that information. Why do you need to know?"

"To get an better understanding of who the man was. One minute he's sitting next to my best friend, alive, the next minute he's dead."

"Let's have that drink, and we'll talk."

CC gave in and made arrangements to meet him. As she hung up, her phone rang. "CC, we have to go to

Atlanta," Anne said into the phone, not giving CC a minute to answer.

"Why?"

"Bernie's estate sale starts tomorrow. I read about it online."

Chapter Thirty

CC was tired. The nearly 12-hour trip in the VW had been exhausting. Her head was aching. In it played a new beat, the resounding ding from Anne's eBay watch list, Ingrid's laughter as Anne and she shared shopping stories, and the engine droning. She almost missed the turnoff for Macon until Anne screamed, "Turn, CC, turn! You almost missed it."

CC swerved onto the exit ramp. An hour later, after a stop for fuel and coffee, they were waiting in line in front of Bernie's house. The line was long and stretched around the side. His house was in a suburban-gated community with its own clubhouse, pool and golf course. It was a new colonial, with white picket fence and green shutters. "What are we looking for?" Ingrid asked.

"We're not sure yet," Anne said.

"Anything related to his travel, importing/exporting business," CC said.

"What would that be?" Ingrid asked.

"I'm not sure yet."

A few minutes later, the line started to move. Several customers were let in. Anne shifted from foot to foot, waiting impatiently. A half hour ticked by, then 45 minutes. Finally, they were allowed in. The three split up. Anne wandered around the main floor, starting in the living room, finding nothing much other than a few golf course watercolors and a Swarovski crystal golf ball paperweight. She went into the dining room which was empty, no furniture, no pretty china, and no crystal.

Then the kitchen. It was apparent that Bernie did not cook much. The cabinets were empty. There was a pile of delivery menus near the fridge. The family room which faced off the kitchen didn't have the look that family lived there, no pictures or paintings, no memories of a life lived.

Upstairs, CC entered the master bedroom. She brushed shoulders with an elderly woman carrying a desk lamp. "Sorry," she murmured. This was a single man's room, the bed was unmade, a pile of clothes lay in a corner, an open suitcase next to it. CC peered in the dresser drawers. Nothing there. She went into the large walk-in closet. Hidden on a shelf in the corner, she found a two-drawer metal file cabinet. Not worth a lot except for what it might tell CC about Bernie. She opened it to see hanging files, one labeled invoices. She quickly closed it and carried the file cabinet to the entry.

Anne found herself in a small room off the family room. Its walls were lined with utility shelves. On the shelves were shipping boxes; there had to be a least a dozen of them. Each one had customs stickers, labeled by country of origin. Anne opened a box. "This room is off limits," a voice said from behind her.

Dropping the box onto the floor, Anne spun around to see a man glaring at her. His hands were on his hips. "Didn't you see the sign?" he asked, pointing to the door, which had a small sign reading *Do Not Enter*.

"No, the door was open," Anne said, scooping up the pashmina scarves that had spilled out, a jewel box of emerald green, ruby red, sapphire blue and her favorite, pink kunzite. She ran her hands through the scarves, feeling their softness. What great Christmas presents these would make. "Are these items for sale?"

"We haven't set a price for the boxes in here. We haven't had time to research them," the man said.

Anne put the scarves back in the box, studied the other boxes on the shelves. "I'd be willing to take the entire lot—room—off your hands," she said. "There must be, what? Twelve boxes here? How about I give you a $50 a box?" She did the math in her head. "That's $600."

"I don't know if I can do that." The man took off his baseball cap and scratched his head. "We should probably research what's inside the boxes first so we can price them correctly."

"I'm taking a gamble here," Anne said, smiling her most persuasive smile. "I could be buying junk. I'm willing to take the risk. How about $800 for the lot?"

"Done," he said. Anne grabbed his hand, shaking it before he changed his mind.

While Ingrid and CC loaded the boxes into the VW, Anne was sidetracked by a pink flamingo in Bernie's backyard. "Anne, some help would be nice," CC called to her.

"Be right there," Anne said, walking instead toward the flamingo. She studied it. She could picture just the spot in her yard, the back corner next to her copper birdbath.

"Anne!" CC called again. This time more insistent.

Anne took one last longing look at the flamingo and went to help CC. When they'd finished loading the van, they headed back out of town. "CC, I think we can sell those scarves at our pop-up sale. We can probably charge at least $60 each for them. And that's just one box."

The entire way home, CC listened to Anne chatter on about the scarves, the boxes and the pink flamingo. Anne restrained herself from diving into the back of the VW and opening each box. She couldn't wait to get home. It was like Christmas. She nodded to Ingrid who reached over the backseat and pulled up one of the smaller boxes. Anne unbuckled her seat belt and crawled to the back next to Ingrid. "What are you doing?" CC yelled, swerving slightly to the right, jostling Anne between the seats.

Anne didn't answer. She ripped open the small box. She held up a small jar of pink crystals. "This is nice. It's expensive," Anne said.

"What is that?" Ingrid asked.

"Himalayan sea salt."

"That's interesting," CC chimed in from the front. "You know, Anne, Himalayan crystal salt is the cleanest salt available on the planet. It was formed about 250 million years ago, give or take a million years, when the sun's energy dried up the original primal sea. It contains all the elements found in our body. Isn't that neat? It's used in alternative health therapy."

Anne thought about drawing a bath when she got home and throwing in a couple bottles. She handed a jar to Ingrid.

"Really, Anne?"

"Sure, that's for you."

Ingrid put it in her small orange Prada bag. Anne reached over and grabbed one of the pashminas and wrapped it around Ingrid's neck. "Doesn't really go with your Def Leppard t-shirt but still looks fabulous on you."

"ORD?" Ingrid read. "All these boxes say ORD? What does that stand for?"

From the front seat, CC chimed in, "That's O'Hare field. Its original name was. . ."

"We know, CC, you already told us," Anne interrupted.

As the Spoon Sisters let that sink in, they drove past Hartsfield-Jackson International Airport. A 747 flew overhead so low Anne almost ducked. "Yeah, Anne, I was thinking the same thing," CC said.

"What were you thinking?"

"I thought we all had a moment there. I was thinking, why would Bernie, who lives less than an hour's drive from one of the country's largest international airports, travel an additional two hours to fly internationally in and out of O'Hare?"

"I don't know. Cheaper airfare," Anne said. It hadn't been what she was thinking about at all. Her mind was on pashminas, salt baths and dinner. There was a good barbecue place on the way home.

"All those boxes with custom tags from Turkey, Zambia, London. They all came through O'Hare," CC said. The rest of the ride home, CC drove in silence, pondering that question. Then the eBay pinging began again.

Chapter Thirty-one

CC and Ingrid trudged up Anne's back snow-covered stairs. They carried box after box, stacking them in Anne's crowded living room. Anne took a break to get her mail. She walked around to the front of the house to the mailbox at the curb, the snow crunching under her feet. She'd have to shovel her sidewalks or she'd get an earful from Grandma Jan. Or even worse, Grandma Jan would be out at 5 a.m. shoveling it herself. She checked her watch, almost midnight.

Anne was very proud of her mailbox. It was an exact made-to-order replica of her house. She opened the double doors and pulled out the mail, having to struggle to get out the package that Alex the mailman had shoved in there. She stood there sorting through the pile, saying to herself, "Bill, bill, oh, 20 percent off at Nordstrom's." That one she put in her pocket. The rest she shoved back in the mailbox to think about another day.

She carefully goose-stepped into her own footsteps to trace her way back. She didn't think she needed boots down in Georgia but the four inches of snow back in Illinois were ruining her Sam Edelman ballet slippers. Left, right, left, right. She tiptoed lightly into her footprints like a ballerina until she reached two lefts. One nearly twice the size of hers. She stopped, looking over her shoulder. Had those footprints been there before? The footprints continued up her stairs to her front porch. She followed the footprints around the wraparound deck to the side of her house. She bent over the railing in time to see the boxwood evergreen bushes shake and sway. She jumped back, holding her heart. "CC!" she screamed in a whisper. "CC," her lips froze.

A shadow passed under the streetlight and was gone. Anne felt a hand on her shoulders. She jumped even higher. "Anne, what are you doing? We're almost done moving the boxes," CC said.

"CC, the bushes." Anne pointed. "There was someone in the bushes."

"Are you sure? It wasn't a raccoon?"

"No, CC, look at the footprints." Anne pointed to the ground.

"Anne, let's get in the house, now." CC put her arm around her friend and led her into the house.

Anne locked the front door behind them. Ingrid was carrying the last box in from the back porch into the kitchen. Anne locked the kitchen door behind Ingrid. "Anne, what's wrong?"

"Better be safe than sorry," Anne said, not wanting to worry Ingrid.

"Anne, why don't you sit down? I'll make us some tea," CC said.

Anne sat under the rescued oak shelf, heavy with antique coffee grinders and a 20-pound Persian. She leaned up against the checkerboard ceramic tile. It vibrated from Sassy's purring above her. The three kittens were sound asleep in the playpen in the corner of the kitchen near the warmest spot by the radiator. CC brought Anne a cup of chamomile tea. "CC, there's some Salerno cookies in the pantry." Anne sipped her tea and then her phone pinged. It was eBay telling her she'd won a $10 biscuit jar.

"Should we start going through the boxes?" CC asked, standing up.

"Yes, let's." Anne perked up.

Anne cleared a space on the couch and watched Ingrid and CC open boxes. The first box was the one full of the pashmina scarves. Anne's anxiety soon disappeared as she watched the kittens wind through the scarves. "These are wonderful, CC. I think we should include them at the next sale. People can buy them for Christmas presents."

"That's a great idea, Anne." CC pulled the scarves back into the box and moved the box towards the back door to make room.

Ingrid tore open the next box labeled Zambia. This one was full of wooden tribal masks decorated in bright reds and yellows. "You know, Anne, we should have these checked out. African tribal masks usually have spiritual and religious meaning. A person's social status is conveyed by the symbols on the mask."

While Anne and Ingrid continued to sort through boxes, CC opened the file cabinet she'd bought. She pulled out invoice after invoice, reading each one carefully. They appeared to be in no particular order. She found invoices from Turkey for the scarves, one from Zambia for the tribal masks, one from London for earlier this year. "Anne, this is the last invoice. Did you buy a box marked London? This is dated back about three months," CC said.

Anne tore through the rest of the boxes and found English china teapots. "These are lovely," Anne said, holding up a hand-painted one with English roses. Bernie had good taste. "Can you imagine flying around the world to buy these beautiful things?"

CC stared at the empty file cabinet. "Strange," she said. "The bottom of the file drawer is shallow." She pulled the bottom drawer all the way out. "Anne, do you have a screwdriver I can use?"

Anne turned from the Russian nesting dolls she was arranging on her mantle. "There should be one in the kitchen drawer. Ingrid, try the large drawer near the sink."

Ingrid came back a few minutes later with a screwdriver and handed it to CC, who pried off the sliding drawer and tapped on the metal floor of the cabinet. It echoed. She tugged on the top of the file bottom. It slid forward revealing a hidden pocket. "Anne, come take a look," CC said.

Anne and Ingrid knelt down next to CC, peering over her shoulder, at first not understanding what they were seeing. CC reached down and pulled out a long black velvet jewelry case. She clicked it open.

Anne gasped. "I know that bracelet." Anne stared at the onyx and diamond panther made to crawl around a woman's arm as if it were stalking its prey. The inside of the box read *Cartier*. "That. That. That's. . ." Anne couldn't speak.

"Breathe, Anne," CC said, putting her hand on her shoulder.

"That. That. It's Wallis Simpson's." Anne gasped out in one long drawn-out breath. "That was up for auction at Sotheby's in 2010. I think." Anne counted on her fingers. "It sold for $9 million. That can't be real. It's probably a replica like the heart stone. Bernie imported nice trinkets but not anything worth this kind of money."

"Why would it be hidden in the bottom of this file?" CC asked. "You said it was at auction in Sotheby's in London?"

"Yes," Anne said. "It went to a private buyer. I watched the auction online."

CC ran and grabbed her iPad mini. She typed in *Wallis Simpson panther bracelet*. "Anne, that bracelet was reported stolen three months ago. Ingrid, what's the date on the invoice from London?"

Ingrid sorted through the papers, scanning for *London*. "It's about three months ago."

"What about the pashminas from Turkey?"

"Those are July of last year."

CC typed in *Ankara, jewel theft* and *July*. "Anne, a 20-carat ruby known as the Star of Islam was stolen. What's the date on Zambia?"

"It's April of 2010."

CC typed in *Zambia, jewel theft* and *April 2010*. "A priceless 30-carat emerald necklace that had belonged to Cleopatra had been stolen from a museum."

Anne listened intently, not quite grasping what was going on.

CC turned to her. "Where's the heart diamond?"

Anne opened her large orange Prada bag and held the diamond out, her hand shaking. "So, you're saying Bernie was an international jewel thief? The man who shook like a little scared rabbit was an international jewel thief?" Anne stopped and thought. Bernie didn't fit the Hollywood image of Robert Wagner in *It Takes a Thief*. "Is that what you're saying?"

"Maybe he didn't steal them but he was obviously transporting them," CC said. "How else do you explain your blue diamond?"

"How come nobody claimed his luggage? Or is looking for the knife?" Anne asked.

"Someone is looking for the knife. The same person who killed the sweet shop lady."

"You're saying the professor didn't kill the sweet shop lady?" Anne asked.

"No, don't you see, Anne? Whoever killed the sweet shop lady wanted the knife. We advertised the knife would be for sale at the pop-up sale. The night before the sale, someone tried breaking into the store, I believe to steal the knife. Steal it because they didn't want their identity to be tied to the knife, so much so, that when the sweet shop lady saw them that night, he killed her. The professor came to buy the desk. He could have easily bought the cake knife if that was what he was after. No, Anne, the professor is not a killer," CC said. "Whoever killed the sweet shop lady killed Bernie. We have to find our more about Bernie? Why is he flying out of O'Hare and not Atlanta? There must be a connection. I'm going to talk to Gregg." CC paused and then said, "You and Ingrid go see Amy. Bring her the bracelet and the blue stone." As CC spoke, the lights flickered and went out. "Anne, did you pay your electric bill?"

Anne stopped to think. "Yeah, I paid a couple months." She lit several candles. "This is actually rather pleasant, isn't it? I like candlelight. It gives me the chance to use some of my candles." She sniffed the earthy fragrance from the one candle. "This is sandalwood." Sassy wound around the candle, sniffing. The kittens trailed behind her like ducklings. "I think Sassy likes the smell, too," Anne said.

Anne turned to go to the kitchen and screamed. The back door shook and rattled. CC and Ingrid made their way into the kitchen, bumping into chairs, boxes and old newspapers. The face obscured by a ski mask disappeared and then the back door was kicked open. Anne screamed. A large figure outlined only by the sliver of moonlight that shined through Anne's kitchen window, reaching for Anne, grabbing her by the throat. She thrashed and kicked but the man would not release his hold. Ingrid pushed the man off Anne. CC grabbed Aunt Sybil's teakettle off the stove and flung its contents at him. The steaming water splashed on his chest and throat. He let out a piercing growl like a wounded animal, swinging wildly at CC. With one last howl, he ran out into the night, clutching his throat. CC slammed the door and jammed the kitchen chair under the doorknob. Anne was already speed-dialing Nigel. He didn't answer.

"We have to get out of here. It's not safe," CC said.

"What's that smell?" Ingrid asked.

"It's smoke." They ran back into the living room. The kittens had knocked over the large sandalwood candle which had caught fire to a pile of newspapers. The living room was now on fire. Anne's vintage William Morris drapes were engulfed in flames. The fire continued up to the ceiling, crawling like a baneful spider over their heads. Anne's beloved 1910 bungalow was a perfect kindle box, full of wood furniture and endless stacks of magazines and papers.

CC grabbed a throw blanket off the couch, trying to put out the fire. Anne ran from the kitchen with a potful of water. The thirsty fire gulped up the water. Ingrid, rounded up the kittens and put them in a box, covering them with a blanket. Anne ran about looking for Sassy.

It was hopeless. All their efforts seemed to stir the intensity of the blaze even further. Anne found Sassy in the kitchen on the shelf above the table. In the distance, they could hear the sirens of fire trucks. The back door kicked open. Grandma Jan in her nightgown burst in, carrying a garden hose. "Anne, get out! The fire trucks are on their way," she called out.

Moments later, they watched from the safety of the sidewalk behind the fire trucks. As the roof caved in, Anne clutched Sassy. By the time the sun came up, the smoldering pile of Chicago red bricks was all that remained of a lifetime of memories. After the fire was extinguished, Anne walked around the wreckage that had been her home. The ruined contents brought back specific memories. This burnt mahogany table had once smelled like summer parties and petite finger sandwiches served to ladies in big flowered hats. The tattered leather bound first edition of *Anne of Green*

Gables had smelled like winter nights by a warm fire and cocoa too hot to drink without first blowing away the steam rising up from the chocolate goodness. "Gone, all gone," she muttered. Anne's knees buckled; CC propped her up. Anne clutched her large orange Prada bag, all that was remaining of her worldly collections.

"Let's go to my house," CC said, leading Anne to the VW. Ingrid was already sitting in the back seat with Sassy and the kittens.

As CC backed the van out of the driveway, Anne took one last glance at the charred remains.

Chapter Thirty-two

The L tracks clacked overhead as Ingrid and Anne skirted the icy slicks down Wabash Avenue, Chicago's Jeweler's Row. A good night's rest and a hearty breakfast shored up Anne's resolve. The police were doing all they could do. Now it was up to her. Well, really CC, Ingrid and her. But if she was truly honest with herself, it was really up to her. She was Nancy Drew, Vicki Barr and Cherry Ames. The pages of her childhood favorite mysteries come to life except the consequences were real. Houses burnt to the ground; people died. No rewriting endings.

Anne stopped at a small storefront. Its sign read, *Collections by Amy*. She pressed the buzzer and the door clicked open. A petite, beautiful young woman came out to greet them. "Anne!" she shouted as she walked through the rows of glass display cases, stopping momentarily and then hugging Anne.

Over her shoulder, Anne spotted a peacock brooch; its colorful plumage held her gaze. "Oh, Amy, so good to see you again."

"I don't see as many of my old friends since I moved downtown. Betsy was in the other day."

Anne mumbled, "Buttersworth."

"And who's this?"

"This is my apprentice, Ingrid, CC's cousin from Germany."

Amy held out her hand. "So good to meet you."

"You have a lovely store. So many beautiful pieces," Ingrid said, glancing around the room at the photos of engagement rings hanging on the wall. "Oh, what's this?" She pointed to one.

"That's a yellow three carat diamond solitaire in a platinum band. It's one of a kind. Once I design a piece, I break the mold," Amy said. "Let's go back." Amy led the way to the back counter. She put out a black velvet cloth on the glass. "Let's see what you have."

Anne turned her attention from the single morganite stone hanging delicately from its rose gold chain in the case. "How much is that?"

"That's a fine piece of morganite. It's getting rarer and rarer to find these days. That piece is $1,800."

Anne thought for a moment as she calculated her monthly bills in her head. "Do you have layaway?"

Amy laughed. "You haven't changed, have you? We can work something out. Let me see the stone you came here about."

Anne pulled the blue stone out of her bag. She set it on the counter with a flourish. "Voila," she said.

"It's beautiful," Amy said. She picked it up and held it to her eye, examining it with her loupe.

"The question is: is it real?" Anne asked, holding her breath.

Amy placed it under her microscope, not saying a word. She reached under the counter and pulled out a machine. "This is a diamond tester. Actually, it's a dual tester. It tests both the electrical conductivity and the thermal conductivity." Amy tested the stone, took a breath and sat down on the tall stool behind the counter.

"What's wrong?" Anne asked.

"Where did you say you got this stone?"

"Oh, it's a funny story. It was inside a souvenir cake knife, a replica of one that supposedly Marie Antoinette used when she said, 'Let them eat cake.'"

"Oh," Amy said. "I've seen this before. Hold on a minute." She ran into the back room and came back carrying a book.

Anne read the cover, *Famous Precious Jewels* and felt her excitement grow. Amy found the page she was looking for and turned the book around toward Anne. The image was a picture of a heart-shaped blue stone set in a gold ring. The caption read, "This blue diamond belonged in Marie Antoinette's private collection. She gave it to Princess Lubormirska. After the princess was killed in the revolution, the ring was rumored to be in private hands until it showed up at Christie's in 1983 where it was bought by a private collector."

"No, no; don't tell me this. Not again," Anne said. "I thought the cake knife was real. Now you're telling me the stone inside the fake cake knife is real and belonged to Marie Antoinette."

"It's a real blue diamond. It's priceless," Amy said. "There's no doubt about it. I can find out if it was reported stolen. The last known owner was in Spain in 2007."

Anne looked around at all the beautiful pieces of jewelry, none of them could compare to the blue diamond, the history behind it, the person who wore it. She was going into overload. The room was spinning. It was too much. She took deep breaths and counted to ten. "Are you okay, Anne? Do you want water?" Amy asked.

"Cake. I want cake. Let me eat cake," Anne said.

"Anne, you're babbling. What's wrong?"

"Cake."

Amy ran from behind the counter. She and Ingrid each took an arm and gently placed Anne in one of the comfortable overstuffed chairs. Amy ran to the back and came back with a bottle of water. "Take a sip, Anne."

"Cake. Let me eat cake."

The kaleidoscope of colors from all the precious gems danced around her head. She could hear the strains of a French minuet. She could taste buttercream. She licked her lips. "Anne," a voice whispered in her head with a slight German accent. "Are you okay? Anne."

"Yes, I'm fine."

"We better get you home to lie down," Ingrid said.

"Stolen, wait!" Anne said. She reached back into her bag and pulled out the black velvet box, handing it to Amy.

Amy clicked it open. Then she looked up at Anne who shook her head. Amy put the loupe to her eye and verified the Cartier mark. "Wallis Simpson."

Anne nodded.

"Anne, where did you get these?"

"It's a funny story. Not really funny but a long story."

"I don't need to know that now. Anne, let me lock these up in my safe. I'll contact the FBI. They can check with Interpol," Amy said.

"My stone. My diamond." Anne's hand reached into the air, grasping for it. She connected with the stone and her fist closed around it. She reached out her hand with the stone to Amy. Amy tried to take it but Anne wouldn't release her grip.

"Anne, let it go." Amy said. "It's okay. It'll be safer here locked up."

"Yes, I know." She released her grip, slumping down into the chair. She looked over at Ingrid. "Can we stop and get a cake on the way home?"

"Yes, of course, Anne."

Chapter Thirty-three

CC sat at the bar at Fitzhugh's Tap, an Irish neighborhood bar like those that dotted almost every corner in Chicago. Gregg was late, and she was anxious. Their last drinking episode hadn't gone well. She ordered a Diet Coke. She sipped through the straw and checked her watch again. She checked her phone for messages. None from Gregg. He was nearly 30 minutes late, and she was growing impatient.

She tried calling but his phone went straight to voicemail. She thought he must be upset with her from their last encounter. Had she led him on? In a way, she had. She flirted with him to get what *she* wanted and he didn't get what *he* wanted. Either way, it was the rule of threes. She made her third phone call and sent her third text message, and she was done. If he was upset with her, that was fine. Too upset to give her the courtesy of a return phone call or text. She was done.

She paid for her drink, buttoned her coat and went back outside. She spotted a Starbuck's across the street. She ran against the wind, clutching her laptop bag. After ordering a Café American, she sat surfing the Internet for any information she could find on Bernie. His website came up as Worldwide Imports. She did a search for their incorporation date, which was July, 1997. Most of his products were wholesale but there was a selection available to the public. She swiped through the inventory: pashmina shawls from Turkey, sheepskin boots from Australia, tribal masks from Zambia and bone china from Sussex. All fine items, top quality, worth traveling around the world for. Bernie had an eye for quality. Every place Bernie traveled a priceless piece of jewelry disappeared. And then the trail went cold—as cold as Bernie. "Who was Bernie?" she asked out loud.

The young tattooed barista shrugged. "I don't know."

CC smiled at him as he walked past her, clearing tables. She cradled her steaming cup in her hands. Bernie was a mystery. Why would a man terrified to fly make it his life's work? Or was he terrified of flying? A man who imported expensive, original products yet his cake knife was a replica. None of it made sense. It wasn't adding up.

CC finished her coffee, closed her laptop and went back outside. The street was dark and empty. She glanced up; the streetlight was out. The fluffy snow had turned into a heavy blinding fall. She felt uneasy. She pulled her coat closer around her. She felt as if she was being watched. She quickened her steps. In the parking lot behind the bar, she ran to her VW. She stopped when she heard the thumping strains of AC/DC *Back in Black* coming from an idling Porsche 911. She paused. Gregg's Porsche 911. He'd decided to show up after all. Two hours late. She started to open her VW door and then thought about Bernie. She went over to Gregg's car, brushed the snow from his window and peeked inside. She couldn't see through the frost. She tapped on the window. He ignored her.

She opened the car door. It reeked of alcohol. She put her hand on his shoulder and shook him. No response. "Gregg, wake up." She shook him harder. His head flew back, and he fell to the ground, his eyes and his throat wide open. Blood stained the new-fallen snow red.

Chapter Thirty-four

After CC finished with the police, she got in her VW bus and headed back to Glen Ellyn. When she got home, Anne was reclining on her chaise lounge, a large slice of coconut cake in her hands. Ingrid was nibbling at a smaller piece.

"CC, have some cake," Anne said.

"No, thanks, I don't want any cake."

"Let me tell you our news." Anne sat up. Before Anne continued, CC threw her overcoat on the hall tree. She turned around and stared at Anne. "CC, what's wrong? You look shook up."

"It's been a bad day."

"Was it that Gregg again? He didn't try anything, did he?"

"Gregg is dead."

"What do you mean dead?"

"He was murdered in the parking lot of the bar where we were supposed to meet."

"What do you mean murdered?"

"His throat was cut."

Anne put her cake down and swallowed hard. "CC, that's horrible. What are we going to do?" Anne asked. "That could have been you."

"Somebody killed Gregg to keep him from talking. I called the police." CC sat down.

"But who?" Anne's question lingered in the air as Ingrid brought CC a glass of wine.

CC drank it straight down and sat down, deep in thought. "We don't know *who* but we do know *why*.

Bernie's death was not an accident. Gregg told me when I called him that the coroner's report stated Bernie died of blunt trauma to the head. They found blood on the edge of the lavatory sink."

"It makes sense. I fell when the plane dipped. Bernie could have easily hit his head on the sink," Anne said.

"Bernie was about 300 pounds by what I saw of him. Maybe a 56 to 58 inch waist."

Anne glanced at her cake and rubbed her stomach. She adjusted her yoga pants. She had dressed herself in more forgiving elastic waists these past few weeks. "CC, what are you saying?"

"An airplane lavatory, even on a 767, is a tight squeeze even for. . ." CC glanced at Anne and her cake and changed her words to, "Me. There's no way Bernie could have hit the edge of the sink. His belly would have hit the sink before his head. Bernie was murdered."

"That's horrible," Anne said, picking up her cake plate again. "Do you think it was the man who broke into my house?"

CC nodded her head. "Whoever killed Gregg killed Bernie. Which means he was on the plane, the same flight we were on."

"And he killed the sweet shop lady?" Anne asked. "He's after the Marie Antoinette diamond. And now he's after me."

"Marie Antoinette diamond?" CC asked.

"Amy confirmed that the diamond is real. She believes it's from Marie Antoinette's personal collection. It was stolen during the revolution," Anne said.

"Wow. That's amazing," CC said before turning her focus back to Gregg. CC thought for a moment. "The murderer was on the plane with us. He killed Bernie for the stone." CC sat on the couch and opened her laptop.

"What are you doing?"

"I scanned all Bernie's invoices and ticket receipts from his flights. On all his other flights, he flew business class. Bernie was frugal. I thought for someone as wealthy as Bernie, his house was modest and he didn't have much furniture."

"And he was wearing a Timex. Why would he wear a Timex?" Anne interrupted.

"Why first class this trip? What was different?" CC found his original receipt for his Paris flight and studied it. "Wait a minute. Bernie wasn't supposed to be on our flight. His original ticket was business class two days later. Our plane was overbooked. He must have changed his ticket last minute at the airport. Bernie had to get out of Paris quickly."

"Of course, he did. Maybe Interpol was after him," Anne said. "He had that priceless diamond."

"If the police were after Bernie looking for the diamond and they didn't find it, they would have questioned the rest of the passengers. We would have been searched. They never would have let us leave the plane," CC said. "Bernie was running from the man who knew the diamond was on the plane. That man put the pieces together like we did. He knew where Bernie traveled and what left with him. He had access to the passenger list and knew your name and that you sat next to Bernie. He was able to get on a fully booked plane at the last minute because Bernie changed his flight."

"That's why Bernie was terrified. He wasn't afraid of flying. He was afraid of whoever was after him," Anne said. "He must have known that man was on our flight because he was out of control. Even the co-pilot tried to calm him down. The flight attendant finally had to go back in coach and get the air marshal to restrain Bernie."

"Coach?" CC asked. "Air marshals don't fly coach. They sit in first class so they can watch the cockpit."

"The co-pilot said he was deadheading." Anne cut herself another piece of coconut cake, this one larger than the first. She licked the icing off the souvenir knife, staring at the hole where the Marie Antoinette blue diamond should have been.

CC grabbed the knife. "I think I know how to find our murderer."

Chapter Thirty-five

It was the week before Christmas. Holiday lights wrapped around the lampposts in downtown Glen Ellyn twinkled. The heavy snow clung to shoppers' boots. All the stores were lit up except for the sweet shop. "Are you sure we need to hold this sale?" Anne glanced at CC as she opened the shop door. "Now that I have all of my money back, is this really necessary?"

"I guess once you receive the money from your homeowner's insurance, you'll be okay," CC said.

Anne hesitated, staring down at her feet. "Insurance. That's not happening," she muttered under her breath.

"What do you mean?" CC asked as they entered the store.

"I'm a little behind on my bills as you know, and my insurance policy lapsed. I was going to pay it right after this sale. Really, I was."

"Oh, Anne, no," CC said.

"CC, it's going to be okay. I have enough to pay off what I owe on the house."

"You still need money to live on. And where are you going to live?"

"I own the land. I can rebuild." Anne thought for a moment. She could live among the remains of her home. No, she couldn't. Sassy wouldn't stand for it. "I guess we should hold this sale. I want to match all these needful things with needful people. That's what Aunt Sybil would have wanted. That's what I want. Plus I'm starting to realize that owning the antiques is not my only pleasure. I love the search, the hunt. And to see the faces of our fans when we find something they've been looking for. I can't really put a price on that, can I?"

Ingrid walked behind Anne, wrapping her arms around her.

It was nearly the end of the day. Anne scanned the shop floor that had been almost sold out. Spoon Sisters fans still flooded in the door. Ingrid brought hot chocolate in Styrofoam cups to those huddling outside in the cold. Anne and CC tried to hurry customers in and out quickly so no one had to wait too long outside.

Anne needed a moment away from the crowd, a chance to breathe, a chance to think. She wandered up the back stairs that led into the attic. The small room had been partially refinished. The original oak floors creaked under her feet. She walked over to the round stained glass window that looked over the street. Even CC's ex-husband couldn't ruin the charm of this old house. She stared at the fans as they waited in line outside the shop. She thought about happy faces as they left with their found treasures. She thought about Dakota, the little girl, she'd met. She thought about Nigel. She glanced around the room, nodded approvingly and thought to herself, what a cozy nest this could be. She headed back downstairs, entering the backroom with its small kitchenette.

Sassy lay on her down feather bed as her kittens tumbled and tossed about her. Anne watched them with a mother's eye, making sure they were safe. She unlatched the baby gate in the doorway and knelt down to pet Sassy. "Well, girl, eight weeks. It's time for the babies to leave the nest. Except I still haven't given you a name yet, have I?" she said as she picked up the fluffy white Persian kitten, the only one of the three with two different color eyes—one blue eye and one green eye. Anne heard a tap in the doorway. She turned to see Nigel dressed like a Dickens' character, scarf wrapped around his neck, top hat and waistcoat. She stared, surprised. Nigel laughed. "Some of the fellows from the squad are singing Christmas carols at the senior center."

Anne rose up off her knees. "That's really nice, Nigel," she said with a sad voice. She turned around and picked up Poppy. "Here she is. She's ready. She's ready to go." Anne cried. Nigel stepped over the baby gate with his long thin grasshopper legs like an Olympic hurdler. He put his arms around her. "Now, now, Anne, she's going to a good home. I'll take great care of her and you can see her anytime."

"It's not the kitten. It's us, Nigel, you don't know how important you are to me," Anne said. "You're more than a friend. I always say we're good friends but it's more than that. You mean so much to me. I'm afraid that if I get too close I'll do something to sabotage our relationship and I'll lose you forever. I don't want that."

Nigel bent over like a question mark, the question being what to say next. He looked Anne in the eyes. "Annie, I had feelings for you the moment I saw you. Those feelings haven't changed. I enjoy spending time with you. I enjoy hearing your laugh, listening to your stories. I think we should put this kettle on to seep, take our time and see what happens. No pressure, no great expectations."

Anne giggled.

"Why are you laughing?"

"You're dressed like a Dickens character and you're talking about great expectations." She reached up and pulled his pencil neck down to her and kissed him on the lips. "I missed you," she whispered.

"How are you set for Christmas eve dinner?"

"No plans for Christmas eve. I usually celebrate Christmas day with my cousin and her kids and CC. And now Ingrid."

"Christmas Eve is a tradition in my family. You might say it's a British thing. Figgy pudding and all. How about this year we share it? I'll give you your present."

Anne's eyes lit up. "Present?"

"Yes, of course."

Anne kissed him again. "It's a date."

Nigel tipped his top hat, placed his hand on his waist and bowed with his best 19th century pose. "For now, we shall leave with anticipation of things that may come. Knowing that the future is bound to the pleasantries we afford ourselves."

"Is that Dickens?"

He bowed again. "No, ma'am; it's Towers." With that, he scooped up the kitten, hurdled the baby gate and went off into the snowy night.

Watching the whole exchange, CC smiled at her old friend. No matter how much Anne denied it, Nigel Towers was the man she was meant to be with. As the last customer left with the last antique, snugly wrapped, CC locked the door and flipped the *open* sign to *closed*. The small storefront was empty. She tallied up the cash register. More than enough to keep Anne and the Spoon Sisters solvent for way into the New Year. One item was left, marked with a *NFS* tag, reserved for a special customer. As Ingrid cleaned up and played with the kittens, CC looked over her handiwork. During the past month of restoring the old building to its original condition, she'd found renewed love for renovation. Even down to the period-correct brass doorknobs, plaster walls, the refinished original oak floors. She was sad to think this would be the last time she would walk about her handiwork. Why, would it have to be? "Ingrid, Anne, come here, I want to talk to you two."

They pulled over two milk crates and sat down, each holding a kitten. "We had a great final sale. I think if we budget right and are very careful, why does this have to be the last sale?" CC asked.

"What are you talking about?"

"I'm talking about this building. This location. It's perfect.'

"Perfect for what?" Anne asked.

"Anne, it's perfect for opening our own antique store."

Anne's eyes sparkled. She looked around the empty room.

"Not just an antique store but think of it more as a store/staging area for our fan list. We can use the blog to share our finds with our fans and have the store for walk-in sales."

"What about inventory? I have nothing left."

CC pulled out her iPhone and scrolled down. "See this list? Since the three sales, our request list has tripled. It's over a thousand requests for antiques, everything from thimbles to Duesenbergs. Why stop now?"

"Really?" Anne said. "What about your job?"

"I can still freelance occasionally but, honestly, this store could support all three of us."

"I can work here full time?" Ingrid asked.

"Of course as long as it doesn't conflict with your school schedule," CC said. "We'll open next week after the holidays. I'll get permits."

There was a tap at the door. They all turned. CC wiped the frost off the stained glass window, glanced out and then opened the door. "I'm sorry but the sale's over," she said.

"That's too bad. I was interested in a couple different pieces. I was wondering if they were all sold." There stood a man in a navy pea coat, scarf wrapped around his neck, the top of his cheeks red from the chill. "If I could, I was looking for a gift for my wife.

She loves to bake. She saw you had an antique cake knife."

CC smiled and opened the door wide. "Please come in. That's one of the remaining items. I think we have time."

He stepped over the threshold and cleared his boots on the mat. He unfolded the scarf around his neck, revealing a peek at scars from a recent burn.

CC glanced at Ingrid who nodded and slipped into the back room. "Please come take a look," CC said, darting her eyes away from the scar. In the small display cabinet lay the cake knife. CC opened the cabinet and handed the knife to the man who examined it.

"Yes, this will do fine," he said. "What's this tag? *NFS?*"

"That means *Not for Sale*," Anne chimed in.

"I don't understand. It's on your sale list on your blog. That's why I came tonight," he said. He looked closer at the green stone. He took out a knife from his coat pocket and dug the stone out. He slowly looked up at CC, still holding his six-inch blade. "Where's the stone?" he growled, reaching for CC.

"The police are on their way," CC said, taking a step back.

"Where's the stone?" he repeated, moving towards her.

"Safe," Anne said, backing toward the door.

"Wrong answer. It doesn't belong to you. It's mine." He brandished the knife in the air.

"Bernie knew you were scheduled to be on his original return flight," CC said. "That's why he left Paris early. He was afraid of you."

"Bernie was just a mule, a carrier pigeon. This thing is much bigger than Gregg and Bernie. Millions of dollars. I took all the risks for little reward. That diamond is my retirement."

"Gregg made sure you were on all of Bernie's flights, watching his back, making sure everything went smoothly," CC said.

"That's right. I cleaned up all their messes until I had to clean them up. I've killed three people for that diamond. You don't think, I'll kill you?" The air marshal grabbed CC and put the blade up to her throat. "Where's the stone?"

Ingrid stepped up from behind him. CC closed her eyes as Ingrid tossed the ghost pepper powder into the air marshal's face. He fell to the floor, clutching his burning eyes. Sirens screamed in the distance.

Chapter Thirty-six

Anne flipped the *closed* sign; their first real day in business had been busy.

Fans seeking to find treasures and to take a peek at the new Spoon Sisters' antique store had kept her running all day. She put her aching feet up on the counter, picking up her phone to check her eBay watch list. Ingrid brought her a cup of tea.

Her phone rang. "Hi, Amy," Anne answered. She listened intently for a few minutes and then hung up the phone, her eyes sparkling, her face flushed.

"That was Amy?" CC asked.

"Yeah," Anne said.

"What did she say?" CC asked.

"She said that the insurance companies for the bracelet and the diamond were very happy to get both back."

"And?"

"I'll be receiving a reward for both of them. A finder's fee. The ultimate killer finds." Anne's eyes lit up. Her mind filled with visions of building her dream house. From the ashes of her 1910 bungalow would arise a magnificent estate.

Ingrid brought her a slice of cake. There was a tap on the door. Anne got up, opened the door. It was her cousin, Suzanne, with her two little girls. "I wanted to see your store," Suzanne said as Anne let her in. She looked around. "The traffic was impossible from Glencoe."

Anne hugged her and knelt down to talk to the girls. "How would you two like to play with a fluffy white kitten?"

"Can we, Mom?" The girls looked up at their mother.

"Of course," Suzanne said.

Anne led the girls to the back room where the last kitten was, knocking over boxes, peeking inside. "Maybe you can help me name her?" Anne asked the girls who nodded.

"Susie, I found something for you and the girls." Anne ran into the open closet door at the back of the storefront. She brought out a small red rocking horse.

"Anne, that looks just like. . ."

"Yeah, the one we played with when we were little girls at Aunt Sybil's. It's from Sweden. It's the same make and year."

"Thank you." Suzanne hugged her. "I've got something for you, too. I couldn't wait." Suzanne ran out, coming back a few minutes later, carrying a package. "I had sent it out to be framed and it wasn't ready at Christmas."

"What is it?"

"Open it."

As Anne tore the paper, she could see the scrolled silver plate frame. "This is a beautiful frame." She carefully unwrapped the remaining silver and gold Christmas paper. She could see a face staring up at her. The eyes locked on her. Anne looked up at Suzanne who smiled back. Anne tore open the rest of the paper. "Suzanne, this is absolutely beautiful." Anne turned the portrait around to show CC and Ingrid, her Great Aunt Sybil Hillstrom in her 1940's satin wedding dress. "I've never seen this before."

"That was Aunt Sybil's happiest day. She had that portrait of her painted in her wedding dress before her fiancé shipped off. It was to be a wedding gift to him when he came back from the European theater in 1944," Suzanne said.

"I never saw any picture or painting of Sybil in her wedding dress after what happened," Anne said. "Where did you find this?"

"I found it in Great Aunt Sybil's attic."

Anne hung it behind the cash register. She stood back and stared at it. "Sybil's eyes follow you when you move." Anne stepped to the left and then to the right, thought a moment, gave an approving nod, and said, "That's the name of our store." She turned around with Great Aunt Sybil peeking out from behind her. "The Spoon Sisters are proud to announce the grand opening of their antique store, Great Aunt Sybil's Attic."

Ingrid and CC nodded. "Cousin Anne, that's the perfect name for your kitten," Jenny, Suzanne's oldest daughter, said.

"What is?" Anne asked.

"Sybil, Sybil, like Great Aunt Sybil."

"Sybil it is," Anne said as she petted the purring Persian.

"Let's go back to the kitchen for hot chocolate," CC said.

"I'll be there in a few minutes," Anne said as the others left the room. Anne stood alone staring at the portrait. This was the beginning of her new life. New year, new opportunities. Great Aunt Sybil would have been proud. Anne whispered to the portrait, "I promise you that all the lost needful things will find a good home."

As Anne turned and headed to the back room, she swore she heard a voice whisper from behind her, "orphaned artifacts."

THE END

ABOUT THE AUTHOR

With a passion for shopping, Vicki Vass drew on her experiences as an antique hunter to tell the story of her real-life friends Anne and CC. This book is the third in their series. The first was entitled *Murder for Sale* and the second was *Pickin' Murder*.

Vicki Vass has written more than 1,400 articles for *The Chicago Tribune* as well as *Women's World, The Daily Herald* and *Home & Away*. Her science fiction novel, *Eleven: 1,* was inspired by her journeys in the jungle of Sudan, Africa, while writing about the ongoing civil war for World Relief.

She lives outside Chicago, with her writer, musician, husband Brian, their 20-year old son Tony, kittens Pixel and Terra, Australian shepherd Bandit, seven koi and Gary the turtle.

www.ingramcontent.com/pod-product-compliance
Lightning Source LLC
Chambersburg PA
CBHW020630180626
46816CB00003B/887